Roman could hear the water running while he locked up the house and turned off lights. Much as he tried to concentrate on anything else, he couldn't prevent vivid images of the woman in the shower from passing through his mind.

He'd entertained houseguests on numerous occasions.

This was different.

No way could he forget that Brit Langford was standing under that water. With clothes on, she was breathtaking. The sight of her without—

Stop right there, Lufkilovich.

Realizing it was going to be a long night, he headed for the kitchen and pulled a can of beer from the refrigerator. He rarely drank anything alcoholic, but tonight he needed something to offset the adrenaline running through his body.

You're losing it, Lufkilovich. That woman has slipped past all your reliable defenses and has somehow worked her way beneath your skin. You're not the same man you were before you took this case.

Dear Reader,

Get ready to meet the world's most eligible bachelors: they're sexy, successful and, best of all, they're all yours!

This month in Harlequin Romance® we bring you the first book in a great new series, BACHELOR TERRITORY. These books have two things in common—they're all predominantly written from the hero's point of view, and they all make wonderful reading!

This month's book is *Undercover Husband* by Rebecca Winters. Every other month we'll be bringing you one BACHELOR TERRITORY book by some of the brightest and the best Harlequin Romance authors. Included in the lineup are Emma Richmond, Lucy Gordon, Heather Allison and Barbara McMahon.

In March it's Val Daniels's turn with #3497 *Marriage on His Terms*.

Happy Reading!

The Editors

There are two sides to every story...
and now it's his turn!

P.S. Look out in Harlequin Presents for our "brother" promotion Man Talk! starting in April with bestselling author Charlotte Lamb.

Rebecca Winters

Undercover Husband

Harlequin Books

TORONTO • NEW YORK • LONDON
AMSTERDAM • PARIS • SYDNEY • HAMBURG
STOCKHOLM • ATHENS • TOKYO • MILAN
MADRID • WARSAW • BUDAPEST • AUCKLAND

ISBN 0-373-03489-X

UNDERCOVER HUSBAND

First North American Publication 1998.

This edition published by arrangement with Harlequin Books S.A.

® and TM are trademarks of the publisher. Trademarks indicated with
® are registered in the United States Patent and Trademark Office, the
Canadian Trade Marks Office and in other countries.

Printed in U.S.A.

CHAPTER ONE ✝

BRITTANY LANGFORD, better known to her friends as Brit, anxiously scanned the hundred or so listings of private investigators in the Yellow Pages of the phone directory. Most of the ads didn't mention stalking. She turned the page where her attention was immediately drawn to one particular advertisement near the bottom.

LFK Associates International. *If you need peace of mind, or simply proof.* * Background Checks * Surveillance * Stalkings * Decoy * Undercover * Security/Bodyguard * Experienced Former Federal Law Enforcement Security * Investigations * U.S. Marine Corps Special Tactical Surveillance Unit.

Brit didn't have to look any further. Everything about the ad and professional credentials felt right to her. No address had been given. She jotted down the phone number, then got up from the table on shaky legs and walked to the phone booth at the rear of her favorite Mexican restaurant.

After a few minutes she heard, "You've reached LFK-5555. May I help you?" a pleasant female voice spoke up.

"Yes. My name is Brit Langford. I—I'm being harassed by a man I met in Europe this summer and I'm so frightened I don't know what to do. Lieutenant Parker of the Stalking Unit at the Salt Lake Police Department is handling my case. He says it's pretty routine, but—"

"But you need further assurance so you won't lose your sanity," the receptionist finished for her.

"Exactly. The thing is, I don't have much money. I can get it. I'll apply for a loan and—"

"Before money is discussed, I need to take down all the pertinent information you can give me. If one of the investigators decides he wants to handle your case, an affordable fee payment plan will be drawn up. How does that sound to you?"

Brit clutched the receiver tighter. "It sounds wonderful."

In the next few minutes she'd told the receptionist every detail she could think of.

"All right, Ms. Langford. I have your phone and work numbers, and the times when you can be reached. No matter the answer, one of the investigators will get back to you before the day is out."

"Thank you very much." To her embarrassment her voice wobbled. "I hope someone there decides to help me."

"I hope so, too. Be expecting a call."

"Ladies and gentlemen of the Nevada Police Academy— with our other business out of the way this morning, I'd now like to present the man you've been waiting to hear from. He's here in Las Vegas for a well-deserved rest after helping mastermind the stakeout which resulted in the capture of the notorious Moffat brothers, two killers who'd managed to elude the best officers in six western states until now."

Ear-splitting applause broke out.

It was part of a front for a top secret, covert operation out in the Nevada desert.

Though it was an operation of which he could approve, Roman had gone from being an idealistic soldier, to a disillusioned officer in the military, to a disenchanted CIA agent.

For a variety of reasons—not the least of which was his distaste for the growing corruption within the system—he was thinking of getting out.

"The man's credentials speak for themselves. After serving in the Marines in a special tactical surveillance unit for a number of years, he went to work as a law enforcement officer with the New York City Police Department."

Correction. My time in the New York City Police Department was another cover to gather information about drug-trafficking coming out of South America. What I found was a number of people within the community of law enforcement who were involved and it has sickened me.

"He's a special agent of the International Police Congress, the Associated Licensed Detectives of New York, Bureau of Missing Children, American Society of Industrial Security, National Association of Chiefs of Police, Academy of Security Educators and Trainers and International Association of Law Enforcement Intelligence Analysts."

But I'm rarely given the time to do the P.I. work I love.

"He founded Professionals International, and at present is the owner, licensee and executive director of LFK Associates International, a private investigation firm located in Salt Lake City, Utah."

That's right. My latest temporary cover until they send me to South America. Maybe I'll retire before that day comes. When I'm no longer associated with a system that isn't doing the job, then I can be exclusive as a P.I. and fight other problems plaguing society right here at home.

"Without further ado, we'll now hear from Lieutenant Roman Lufka."

Another burst of applause accompanied Roman's short walk to the rostrum. He looked around his audience of a couple of hundred law enforcement people.

For the most part, *this* group in front of him—whether on or off duty—were hardworking, law-abiding citizens themselves, the cornerstone of goodness in the whole scheme of police work.

Unfortunately, the higher one climbed, be it a member of the FBI or the CIA, there was a tendency to get bogged down by a corrupt bureaucracy.

Roman. You're tired...

"It seems the only thing Chief Wilson didn't tell you is that the name written on my birth certificate reads Romanov Vechiarelli Lufkilovich. My great-grandparents on my father's side were Russian immigrants who arrived and settled in New York. My mother's people were of Italian ancestry who also settled in New York.

"When I came home from grade school with my tenth nosebleed in a row, my parents agreed to let me shorten my name to Roman Lufka, which incorporated a little of the best parts of all the blood flowing through my veins.

"Of course by then, I'd begun to learn how to take care of myself. The other guy ended up in the hospital. I suppose I have my parents to thank for putting me on the road to my particular and peculiar destiny, no matter how ignominious and self-serving its start."

A roar of laughter filled the conference room. Someone called out, "How come you ended up in Salt Lake?"

If you only knew...

"That's an interesting question," Roman responded when quiet reigned. "Would you believe, skiing? The rumors are true. Utah has the best snow on earth. To *this* New Yorker anyway," he added with a smile.

That part was true. The skiing was fabulous. He was already addicted...

Judging by the shouts and whistles, a large portion of the audience agreed with him.

"I could go on all day about my favorite sport. However, Chief Wilson has a reputation, if you know what I mean, and he expects us to get some work done here."

Again the room exploded with good-natured guffaws and laughter.

"As you know, in the past, the image of the private investigator hasn't been the best. I'll be the first to admit that incompetent bunglers, less-than-professional idiots who couldn't find their way out of an unlocked closet, have riddled our noble profession with holes which the media has picked up on and exploited in the worst possible light.

"We've been made out as uninformed, uneducated riff-raff, rising from the dregs of society in our rumpled clothes which wreak of cigarette smoke and garlic from yesterday's leftover pastrami sandwich eaten out of a rundown '72 Chevy we haven't finished making payments on. The exhaust pipe, by the way, long since confiscated by local hoodlums.''

Again everyone laughed and clapped in agreement because the picture he painted was too real and hit too close to home.

"I'm here to tell you that this image is changing. No longer is there room in the private investigation field for those of us choosing this line of work to be anything but professional. In fact, we're approaching the year 2000 where we'll be wiped out, eliminated from the competition, unless we become the absolute, total professional.

"This means you have to be dedicated to a higher degree of commitment as you study and learn everything possible to navigate and win in our specialized and technical society. As crime spreads like the incurable ebola virus, mutating in hideous new forms, we have to be equipped to handle the awful and unprecedented tasks besetting us, testing us to the last atom of our cognitive thinking powers.

"That's what being professional is all about. That's why I'm here today, to provoke you to be better than you've ever been before, to reach inside that core of you which will not stand for mediocre or slovenly service, but will respond to the highest call to be your brother's keeper in the noblest sense of the word, defending the helpless, even to the giving of your own life, if necessary.

"But the chances of that happening diminish in direct ratio to the degree of your professionalism, and that's a fact you can take to the bank.''

There was absolute quiet before the room suddenly erupted into thunderous ovation. When Roman could get a word in he said, "That's it. That's my speech. I'd rather turn the rest of the time over to a thirty-minute question and answer period before I have to get back to Salt Lake on the noon flight.''

"Another call on line two, Brit!" the secretary spoke up.

Brit's gaze darted to the wall clock. Ten after three. Maybe this was the one she'd been waiting for.

She left the drafting board and rushed over to her desk. "Brit Langford, here."

"Ms. Langford. This is Diana from LFK."

Her heart plummeted to her feet. Maybe the receptionist was calling to tell her they wouldn't be able to take her case.

"Y-yes?" she answered, dry-mouthed.

"Hold on. I'm putting you through to Lieutenant Lufka."

Brit gripped the receiver more tightly.

"Ms. Langford? Roman Lufka here. From what my secretary, Diana, has told me, it sounds as if you've got a serious problem on your hands."

The deep cultured voice whose accent suggested an East Coast education and sophistication came as much of a surprise to her as his assurance that her fears were justified. The police had shown her relatively little interest or compassion.

"I get a pit in my stomach just anticipating looking at the mail. When the first letter came, I thought it had to be some sort of hideous joke, but it has gone on too long. I was feeling so desperate I decided to call your office."

"I'm glad you did. Can you meet me at Lieutenant Parker's office in say, twenty minutes?"

She breathed a huge sigh of relief. "Oh, yes. Does this mean you'll take my case?"

"It does."

"Thank you." Her voice trembled.

"You're welcome. See you soon."

She heard the click before she put the receiver back on the hook. *Thank goodness she was going to get some help.*

*   *   *

Roman drove the tan Ford he used on the job into the underground carpark of the metropolitan hall of justice.

Unfortunately, there was no anonymity here. By the time he'd reached the third floor of the complex, he'd shaken hands with a dozen officers and exchanged shoptalk with a dozen more who wanted to discuss the stakeout he'd been on.

He broke it off as soon as he could and headed for Parker's office. The head of the stalking bureau possessed a need to be in control at all times. Since he was on the phone, Roman used sign language for permission to get into the files. The other man hesitated, then expelled a frustrated sigh and nodded his go-ahead.

On his way to the cabinet, Roman theorized that this had to be one of Parker's better days, or else the phone call had distracted him.

His client hadn't arrived yet. He decided to get started.

Lam, Lamoreaux, Landau, Landrigan, *Langford*. Roman pulled her file and sat down at a table against the wall.

The first item to meet his gaze was a copy of her passport photo, and a large color photograph of her tour group assembled on the steps of St. Peter's in Rome.

A hairy-faced figure among the group had been circled with black marker. Obviously he was the man who'd been harassing her.

Roman's eyes darted to the other people in the crowd until he found Brittany Langford, a budding new architect according to Diana.

With her ash-blond hair long enough to be pulled back in a medium-size ponytail, she looked about nineteen rather than twenty-six, and very attractive.

Putting the pictures aside, he began studying the information from the report taken by investigating Officer Green. It was sparse at best.

Glen Baird. White male, approximately six feet, medium build, medium-dark brown hair and brown eyes, resident of Madison, Wisconsin.

If the man's hair were shaved off, the description could belong to hundreds of thousands of men in the U.S. The letters would tell Roman a great deal more.

Oftentimes it was during the initial perusal of evidence—when his brain seemed to be in free-association mode—that his creative side took over. As ideas sprang into his mind—ideas to be followed up on at a later date—he would make verbal notes into his pocket recorder.

The process of assessing, digesting, analyzing random bits of information generally revealed a pattern, sometimes a whole picture of a mind that didn't function in the normal way.

He started to pull the recorder from his pocket when he heard his name called out in a familiar feminine voice with that slightly husky tone. He looked up to discover that his newest client was even more beautiful than the picture had revealed.

Those vibrant blue eyes and flawless young skin, all part of her classic features, would draw any man's gaze. But combined with the full curves of her figure and long slender legs the blouse and skirt couldn't camouflage, she would definitely be the star attraction anywhere, let alone on her tour bus.

"Ms. Langford." Rising to his feet, he put out his hand for her to shake, then flashed her his credentials to identify himself.

The top of her head reached his chin. A subtle, flowery fragrance emanated from her.

As a rule, when Brit tried to match a face with a voice, she was totally off base and inevitably disappointed. For once in her life, the reality surpassed the image of the bodyguard-type she'd conjured in her mind.

His hazel eyes stared directly into hers. The attractive, dark-haired man stood at least six feet two, maybe three. He had a lean, powerful build and was probably in his mid- to late-thirties. With a name like that and his olive complexion, he was definitely of European or even Eastern

European extraction. Yet he was as American as she was. The combination took her breath.

There weren't any men of her acquaintance who looked remotely like him, not even a few of the striking foreign males she'd met on her tour.

Her gaze quickly reverted once more to his company credentials which contained his picture and description.

"Please. Sit down."

"Thank you."

He helped guide her to a chair before he sat opposite her. There was an air of unreality about the whole situation. What in heaven's name was wrong with her?

"I appreciate your being willing to talk to me this afternoon, for making it possible for me to pay you in installments. I'm very grateful." *Damn*. Her voice quivered.

"It's my job," he murmured with a quick smile. That, plus his attire of polo shirt and chinos, gave him a humanness lacking in the uniformed police officers she'd talked to thus far. Brit wished she could achieve the confidence and calm he exuded.

"From what Diana told me on the phone, you've never been in this kind of a situation before. A virtual stranger has invaded your life totally unsolicited. I don't blame you for being frightened."

"It's horrible." Her voice wobbled again. "Have you read the letters?"

"Not yet. I only arrived a few minutes before you did. Let me look through them first. I'll be using a tape recorder, making verbal notes. Will that bother you?"

She'd been watching him, fascinated by his totally male aura and professional demeanor. "No. O-of course not," she stammered.

"Good."

Roman spent the next few minutes perusing the first of six letters written on lined paper a student would use.

Brittany—

Everyone on the tour called you Brit, but when I saw your full name on the address sheet most of the people signed, I realized that I preferred your full name and plan to call you that. It has a French origin. I know because I spent time in France several years ago.

I have lots of pictures of you, even from behind. I recognize your backpack. What was the name of that shampoo you use? I didn't write it down. Was it, Swiss Formula? I ordered that polka tape from the library. I'm just getting over the flu. How's Denise? Ask her to give me her address and phone number. I want yours, too, so I don't have to sit down and write letters.

In regard to the stuff I've sent in this letter, the Salt Lake Youth Hostel was a supplemental accommodation which means it lacks one or more basic elements of a hostel. It was open when I came through Salt Lake before. It couldn't be much more than eight miles from your place. Some of the hostels listed on the map I've enclosed are no longer open.

This is what's new. I heard yesterday that my section at work is closed until there's more funding which reading between the lines means I'll probably be off work longer. Tuesdays are my rest days, so I will have enjoyed fifty-three days of happiness. Waiting for your letter.

> Until later, much love,
> Glen Baird
> 5972 Washington Court,
> Madison, WI 53701

Roman read through the others and made a few brief comments into the mike, alternately appalled and fascinated by the disjointed, too intimate personal remarks interjected at random. Each letter became progressively angrier because it was obvious she hadn't responded to anything.

Finally he lifted his head, focusing his gaze on her once

more. Brit met his level glance. Since reading the letters, his eyes seemed to have darkened a fraction.

"You're right. Considering that these letters are from a virtual stranger, they *are* terrifying."

"But Lieutenant Parker said—"

"Forgive me for interrupting—" He lowered his voice. "The police get so many calls from people being harassed, it's difficult for them to do a detailed investigation unless the situation warrants it, unless there's an implicit threat to the victim."

"And my case isn't like that."

"Let me finish looking at everything before I answer that question," Roman murmured, applying himself once more to the task.

The papers smelled of lilies. He picked up a plastic bag containing two dilapidated-looking trumpet lilies.

"Those came in that Express Mail overnight letter this morning, along with the sympathy card. He obviously received my postcard."

Roman's head flew back in consternation. "What postcard? I see no mention of it in the report."

"The one the investigating officer suggested I send to him, telling him I was getting married."

"Are you?" he fired back.

"No. I don't even have a boyfriend right now."

With a woman as intelligent and attractive as she was, it seemed a little hard to believe.

"The officer thought a note like that might discourage him," she continued to explain. "I picked a card with Sego Lilies on the front. They're the state flower. I thought it would be impersonal, that he wouldn't be able to read anything into it."

Roman's lips thinned. To some weirdos, that would send up a red flag like nothing else.

His reaction produced a moan from her. "It was the wrong thing to do, wasn't it? *I knew it.*"

"Let's not worry about that now."

He picked up the sympathy card, which smelled heavily of the flowers.

Those we hold most dear, never truly leave us.
They live on in the kindness they showed, the comfort they shared,
And the love they brought into our lives.
May beautiful memories give you strength in those difficult hours ahead.

Beneath the printed words on the inside was a line written in the man's own hand. "I will write you no more. Forever!"

The man writing this was acting like an adolescent who couldn't handle rejection. Between the lines Roman could read the hurt.

His hand reached for the letter folded inside the card. Unlike the others, this one was white type paper with pasted pieces of printed text to form the author's macabre message. Each piece was a different shade of white, indicating he'd gotten his material from many sources.

Brittany—
The language of flowers may be combined and arranged to express the nicest shades of sentiment.

Moss rosebud and myrtle a confession of love.

White, pink, canary and laurel, your talent and perseverance will win you glory.

Mignonette and colored daisy, your qualities surpass your charms of beauty.

Columbine and lily, your folly and coquetry have broken the spell of your beauty.

Did you know red rose means love, yellow rose friendship, white rose fear, pink rose indecision, green rose I'm from Mars, lily I'm dead, Crabgrass I just escaped from a mental institution, scallion I'm clueless.

If a flower is offered reversed, its direct signification

is likewise reversed so that the flower now means the opposite.

Throughout the morass of cryptic lines, the word "lily" kept reappearing. Roman pondered the entry again.

"'Lily, your folly and coquetry have broken the spell of your beauty.'" He spoke out loud, feeling her eyes on him. "We can assume this was the author's way of telling you he couldn't handle your rejection."

"The postcard made him furious." Her voice shook.

Roman nodded. "I agree." His gaze darted to the next lily entry. "Lily means, I'm dead."

His frown deepened. But it was when he reread the last line that his heart did a drop kick. "If a flower is offered reversed, its direct signification is likewise reversed so that the flower now means the opposite."

He raked a hand through his hair. *The opposite of I am dead...*

His eyes sought the plastic bag and he opened it. Two dead lilies stared up at him. But the petals had been folded downward.

If the flower is offered reversed, the flower now means...*you're* dead.

Roman absently tapped the paper against his cheek. This guy was definitely certifiable. But whether he was really dangerous, or just enjoyed threatening his victims, remained to be seen.

To his shock, he was rocked by a savage, unprecedented desire to make certain the lovely woman sitting across from him wouldn't suffer any more fear at the stranger's hands.

Already a plan was forming in his mind. Where the idea came from he had no clue, unless it had leaped straight from his gut. Some primeval instinct was warning him this was no ordinary case, nor she no ordinary woman. Diana had sensed the same thing when she'd begged him to take it, rather than give it to one of the other P.I.s.

Though he doubted that this psycho would actually do more than harass her, Roman could never rule out the possibility that Baird meant what he said. If so, Brittany Langford needed help, and she needed it *now*.

"What are you thinking?" she asked in an anxious voice.

Roman closed the file, schooling his features to show no emotion. "I need to do a little preliminary work first. Are you going home to stay?"

"Yes—"

"Then expect me around seven and we'll talk."

"All right." She got to her feet. "I—I'll see you then."

He watched her progress from the room, unconsciously admiring the singing lines of her body while he put everything back in the drawer. With a swift motion he closed it, a little too soundly because it drew Parker's attention.

"Find what you were looking for?"

"Heaven forbid, I did," Roman ground out.

"It's a mail harassment case, nothing more. One of these days the guy will give up."

That's why you never made chief, Parker.

The man despised private investigators, especially Roman, the outsider from New York City. But he didn't have the courage to call him something uncomplimentary to his face.

"Just doing my job according to Hoyle."

Roman knew his response would pass over the top of Parker's head. Maybe in six months he'd figure it out. By that time, Brittany Langford could be in serious trouble if her tormentor had the potential for menace.

Once he returned to his office, Roman would fax Pat Flaherty in New York. Pat and he had been partners way back when life had been vastly different, when Roman was still full of noble ideas about changing the world...

The cocky Irishman was still on the force and had active contacts who could put out feelers on Glen Baird in a matter of minutes. Roman had one concern at the moment. To find out if Baird still resided in Wisconsin.

CHAPTER TWO

WHEN the doorbell rang a little after seven, Brit knew it was Lieutenant Lufka. For some unaccountable reason, her heart began to hammer. She'd been counting the minutes until he arrived, wondering what conclusions he'd come to about her case.

Oddly enough she'd been loathe to leave the police station. *To leave him.* He engendered such a strong feeling of safety, she found that she didn't want to be out of his sight.

After one brief meeting it was ridiculous to feel that way, but she couldn't help it. The situation with Glen Baird had been going on almost a month. Her nerves were shot. It was heaven to be able to pour out her fears to someone like the Lieutenant who protected people for a living.

She hurried across the living room and opened the door to her condo. He nodded with a hint of a smile, making her feel a little breathless.

"Come in." She stepped aside as he entered, then shut the door behind him. He brought the faint nip of the Fall night air with him. It mingled with the scent of the soap he used, bringing her to a strong physical awareness of him.

Startled by this reaction, she knew she sounded too brusque when she asked him if he'd like a drink or coffee.

"Maybe later," he murmured, taking the upholstered chair opposite the velvet couch after she sat down.

Brit clasped her hands nervously. "Did you find out any new information?"

He nodded, sending her a penetrating glance. "You have every right to be alarmed."

She had trouble swallowing. "So what are you saying?"

He eyed her soberly for a moment. It made her heart skip

19

a beat. "You're paying me your hard-earned money. This means I have to call the shots as I see them without wasting any time."

She could read between the lines. Perspiration broke out on her hairline. "I'm in danger, aren't I?" Her voice shook.

"It's only a feeling on my part, but I believe you *could* be."

Brit moaned and stood up, rubbing her arms with her hands to get the circulation going.

"I've done the preliminary work. There's no warrant out for his arrest in any of the counties in the State of Wisconsin. But he does have a long history of disturbing the peace, disputing with his neighbors, torturing animals who've had the audacity to cross his path.

"He was recently fired from his job for creating trouble with other employees and damaging some merchandise in the warehouse where he worked. His last known address was a trailer court in Madison, but he moved out of there a week ago and drove off in a vintage maroon van with everything he owned."

The Lieutenant had learned that much already? Brit was in awe of him, and more horrified than ever to think that lunatic wasn't anywhere to be found.

"I have a plan, Ms. Langford, but we'll have to move fast."

Her fear was so great, she could scarcely form words. "What plan?"

He stared at her through narrowed eyes. "The one you put into play when you sent him that postcard. In my opinion, you were given the wrong advice. But since it's a *fait accompli*, we'll turn it to our advantage."

She shook her head. "I don't understand."

"It's a long shot. But if my hunch is right and he's headed here, we'll be able to catch him and prevent him from doing this to anyone else. If I'm wrong, and he's just another loser who has finally tired of sending you letters because he's become obsessed with someone else, then no harm has been done. Either way you'll achieve peace of mind, which is my job to give you, leaving us both satisfied.''

Peace of mind...

That meant everything. That's why she'd sought a private investigator in the first place, wasn't it?

Her womanly intuition told her that if this man couldn't provide it, no one could.

She lifted her head and faced him squarely. ''Since those letters started coming, I have to admit I haven't felt safe. Until something's done about him, I'll never feel safe again.''

A strange silence filled the room. He rose to his full height, his intelligent eyes with their black lashes never leaving hers.

''No plan is infallible, but the one I've conceived guarantees I won't be leaving your side until the culprit is caught, or goes away for good.'' He paused. ''For this assignment, I'm going undercover as your husband.''

A thrill of emotion totally foreign to Brit shot through her body. She started to tremble.

His dark brows knit together. ''Before you fall apart on me, hear me out.''

''I'm listening,'' she said in a quiet voice.

He put his hands in his pockets, studying the refined features of her upturned face. ''We don't know if he has done this kind of thing to another woman before, but I would imagine he has.'' She shuddered at the prospect. ''If he has set up some elaborate scheme, it might take weeks, even months, for him to carry it out.''

''*Months*?''

He nodded. ''If you recall, he told you he wouldn't write you again. It could be a bluff, and he's going to wait until you think he's forgotten about you before he makes another move.

''If that's the case, I need a justifiable reason to be around you twenty-four hours a day. Marriage will accomplish that, protect your reputation and allow both of us to get on with other work we need to do at the same time.''

She couldn't argue with his reasoning.

''On the other hand, this might be over in a matter of days. According to what you told me earlier, you are single, and don't have a serious boyfriend. Thus it means that on your tour, no one heard mention of a man in your life, let alone a fiancé.

''Glen Baird knows this. When he received the postcard telling him you were making plans to be married, he knew you were lying.''

Brit nodded.

''Don't forget you rejected him throughout the five week tour. Then you ignored his letters. According to the report you gave Officer Green, none of the acquaintances on your tour bus would give him your phone number. He couldn't reach your best friend, Denise Martin, the woman who went on the tour with you. All doors were closed to him. When he finally received the postcard which told him goodbye forever, he couldn't take the rejection.

''Unfortunately, it's my belief that your message represented something else. You betrayed him with a cheap lie, and so doing committed the unpardonable. Now you have to pay for the sin of not loving him. What we don't know is whether or not the lilies and sympathy card represented the zenith of his rage.''

Everything Roman Lufka was saying made a horrible kind of sense. Her stomach clenched in fear.

He cocked his head to one side. ''That's the quandary, isn't it? Waiting for the game to begin or be over... Isn't that why you called my office? Because the suspense is killing you?''

His questions demanded bald honesty from her.

Brit nodded again, and thought she saw a glimmer of satisfaction in the depths of his eyes.

''If he feels further retribution is necessary, then it's only a matter of time before you're made aware of it. He may or may not decide to come to Salt Lake. He could appear at your condo, or at work, or just follow you around for a long time, showing up at places you least expect. Though he's probably harmless, the fact that he hasn't yet given up on you means you're going to continue to be frightened.''

She was starting to feel sick to her stomach.

"Unfortunately this is the time where most victims make their mistake. They don't want to believe such a thing could happen, so they don't plan ahead and often become immobilized by fear." His voice had dropped to a lower register.

It sent another shiver down her spine.

"That's where I come in. My job is to set a trap for him in case he decides to come to Salt Lake. He has already demonstrated that he's cunning enough to trick you with the mail by sending it from various other states or even countries.

"I hope I'm wrong, but it's my opinion that postcard probably upset him enough to make him want to see you in person. In his twisted mind, if he can't wring a response out of you through the mail, then he's going to make sure you pay because he knows you didn't tell him the truth.''

She bit her lip. "I regretted sending that postcard the minute I slipped it in the letter drop. To be truthful, I've been terrified of him suddenly appearing on my doorstep, or worse, watching me without my knowledge."

"Unless I miss my guess, he'll come. If he's angry enough over your lie, he'll arrive here soon."

She buried her face in her hands. "I think he will, too."

Brit had been going over this in her mind until she couldn't function anymore. That's why she'd sought help. Roman Lufka was a professional. If he thought this was the best way to handle it, then she needed to place her faith and trust in him. But—

"Mr. Lufka?"

"Roman," he came back swiftly. "The sooner you start thinking of me as a husband, the better."

Adrenaline made her body surge.

"Roman—I don't have the kind of money it would take for long-term protection."

He frowned. "Let's get something straight, Brit. That's what I'll be calling you from now on," he added in an aside. "If my suspicions are right, he'll make his move soon, so let's not worry about the money angle right now.

"To those observing from the outside, ours will be the epitome of the loving marriage. On the inside, we'll be friends, and one of the other P.I.s will always be assigned to guard you when I'm not there. We'll share everything except the bedroom. That means cooking, cleaning. I plan to get my money's worth, so let's agree not to talk about it again.

"When this is all over and we've caught him, you can explain the truth to everyone, that you're not married, and life will get back to normal."

Another silence ensued before Brit ventured, "Have you ever gone undercover as a husband before?"

"No. But I've done just about everything else."

"I—I've never been a wife."

"The way you're worrying, you sound like one already. I'm certain you'll get the hang of it, given enough time." The teasing mockery in his tone didn't escape her, but then he grew sober.

"If Baird is on his way here right now, we don't have a lot of time. Playing the part of your husband makes the most sense because it gives me the optimum ability to keep you safe until we find out exactly what he's up to.

"If you don't feel you can go along with my plan, you're welcome to approach another P.I. I'll be happy to refer you to several with outstanding credentials. The decision is yours. Remember that a P.I. operates according to the way he or she sees a case. I have to do it my way, or not at all."

Though his conditions disturbed her in ways she was

reluctant to identify out loud, Brit had to admit she looked upon Roman Lufka as a savior.

"I-if you can make the boogeyman go away forever," she whispered, "I'm willing to commit to your plan, whatever it is."

"Good. Now tell me about Glen Baird."

She'd just made the monumental decision to pretend to a bogus marriage, yet he behaved no differently than before. For an undercover investigator, this was all part of a day's work.

Brit wished she could view it the same way. After all, he wanted to protect her the best way he could. As her husband, he had the legitimate right to be with his wife day and night.

When she really thought about it, his plan was ideal. She'd be a fool to worry about anything else when she believed him to be a totally honorable man. After all, she'd come to him asking for *his* help, not the other way around.

"Glen Baird is the kind of man who says and does whatever he wants, whenever he feels like it," she began. "On the trip he kept trying to sit by me, and he'd follow me everywhere. People on the tour instinctively started crowding around me so he couldn't have access.

"But when we reached Paris, several of them left our tour. I know it was because of him."

Now that she'd gotten started talking, she couldn't seem to stop. "He was moody, and didn't appear to like the tour. None of us could figure out why he'd come. He had a powerful set of binoculars. Sometimes they'd be trained on me from a distance. It was awful."

"That's another piece of information that wasn't in Officer Green's report. What else do you remember?"

"I'm not sure. Early on, Denise and I considered joining another tour, as well, but because of the wonderful Australian friends we'd made en route, we decided to ignore him as best we could and enjoy the trip anyway.

"That was the difficult part. The first time I saw him

loitering in the lobby of our London hotel, he just stared at me out of blank eyes. With all that hair on his face, he scared me.''

Taking a shuddering breath she cried, "I wish to heaven Denise and I had obeyed our first instincts and left the tour.''

A murmur of compassion escaped his lips. "If your guide had had any idea of the terror you're going through right now, I'm sure she'd regret having given everyone free access to the names and addresses of the people on your bus. But it's done now, and chances are he would have found another way to get to you.

"Let's thank providence you had the wisdom to obey your instincts this time and get help. If and when he comes to Salt Lake to look you up, he'll meet with a surprise he wasn't planning on.''

Brit shivered at the chilling sound of his voice.

After a brief pause he said, "If he follows the profile, and I happen to believe he does, he's lost all concept of the guidelines normal people live by. According to his letters, he's been to Salt Lake before. Sending you brochures of hotels near your condo, plus his old map of Salt Lake, circling the street where you live, was his way of telling you that he knows all about you, that you're not going to escape him. He believes he's invincible, and has only one thought—to make you suffer as he has perceived *you've* made *him* suffer.''

Her eyes played over his well-formed features, noting the lines of experience around his mouth. He sounded so sure. "You're the one whose credentials are listed in the Yellow Pages. It's *your* company, isn't it?''

A flash of white teeth unexpectedly set her pulse tripping. "Guilty as charged. There are twelve of us.''

"Have you covered a lot of these kinds of cases?''

Oh, sweetheart. You don't have a clue.

"Too many,'' came the grudging admission. "But let's not dwell on that. We have a wedding to plan. Guests to invite. One of the P.I.s will serve as the minister. We need to talk to your parents and explain the situation.''

At that pronouncement her head reared back, swishing her hair over her shoulders. He moved so fast she couldn't keep up with him.

"My parents don't know anything yet. I've been afraid to tell them for fear of upsetting them. Dad has heart trouble."

"We'll proceed carefully. When they learn the truth, they'll probably be more amenable to my plan. In any event, your parents are going to have to know, because tonight you'll be staying with me," he said in an authoritative voice.

At her startled look he explained, "Before I rang your front doorbell tonight, I checked out your back door and windows. I could have gotten in any of them without your being aware of it. If I could do it, so could he."

Brit had no idea Roman had been wandering around outside her condo.

"Some voyeur types like to enter their victim's premises and look at their personal things, touch them, even steal some of them to make a shrine. Baird mentioned your shampoo because he likes the smell of your hair." *So do I.* "He might want to take something like that as a remembrance."

"That's *horrible!*" The possibility that Glen Baird could creep into her home anytime he wanted almost paralyzed her with fear.

"Safety isn't the only issue. If we're going to make your impending marriage look real to everyone, except your family and Denise who will already know the truth, then it's probable you'd be making preparations to set up residence with your future husband.

"Assuming your tormentor is en route to Salt Lake, the fact that you've changed addresses will lend credence to your claim that you're getting married. To make it stick, you'll have to give your landlord notice. It's possible Baird will case the complex first, even talk to people to learn your habits. I'll have a mobile unit here on guard day and night, monitoring his activities on tape to give to the police."

A shiver racked her body. "After what you've just told me, I'll be glad to get out of here so Glen can't find me, but I've signed a year's lease. I was going to renew it in December."

"If my hunch pays off, this man will make an appearance shortly. We'll be ready for him and you'll be able to resume your normal life without too much delay. In the meantime, my firm will take an option on your place so you can move back in after everything is over. At that point, we'll explain things to your landlord so that you won't lose any money."

He thought of everything! "W-where do you live?"

"In Olympus Cove."

One of her favorite neighborhoods situated at the base of the mountains.

"Don't you have a family?"

"No. I'm on my own. Why don't you call your friend, Denise? Since she was on the tour and Glen Baird mentioned her in the letter, she's involved, too, and needs to know the truth. I'd like to talk to her tonight. She might be able to remember something important to the case."

"She's home tending her younger brother while her parents are away on a trip. What about him? I don't want him frightened."

"He won't be. You can introduce me as your fiancé."

"But he knows I don't have a boyfriend."

A mysterious gleam entered his eyes. "You do now. Tell him I'm the man who once stole your heart, then moved away. Now I'm back to reclaim you."

This time she felt a quickening inside her, and had the strongest conviction that if he had been her old boyfriend, and had moved away, he might very well have gone off with her heart.

"See if it's convenient for us to visit Denise before we

drop by your folks. You can call them from her house and alert them that we'll be over around nine tonight.''

Within five minutes they were on their way across town to Federal Heights where both the Martins and her parents lived. En route she was once again seized by the enormity of the decision she'd just made. Only fear could have caused her to enter into a bogus marriage with a stranger, never raising any major objections.

"You probably think I'm the world's greatest coward,'' she blurted in panic.

He sucked in his breath. "On the contrary, any woman who is working in a male-dominated profession like architecture couldn't possibly be lacking in the courage department.''

Her gaze fastened on him. "You're one of the few men I've ever met who had any understanding of what it's been like for me.''

"Maybe that's because in my profession, I have to be a student of human nature. To do my job right, it's imperative I get close to my clients, whether male or female. So close, I can tell what they're made of, what strengths and weaknesses form their character. That way I can do my best to protect them. Rest assured I respect your fear, Brit.

"*You're* the one who was trapped with that man for five weeks, sensing he wasn't normal. I'm convinced God has instilled different survival instincts in a woman. Fortunately those instincts drove you to seek help.''

After a thoughtful pause she said, "Then those same instincts are telling me you're too good a private investigator to take on just any case. What do you know about this man you haven't told me? Imagination has a lot to answer for as the saying goes.'' She lowered her head. "I need to hear the whole truth.''

So help me, I need the answer to that question myself. "That's the hard part, Brit. I've given you the facts. What I'm going on now is like flying blind with no radar.''

She sighed. "I know what you mean. When I'm trying

to solve a problem of space and design, and I've exhausted every known possibility, sometimes I just have to start playing around, not knowing what I'll find, but not satisfied until the answer is staring me in the face.''

His mouth quirked. "How well I know what you're saying. You've put it better than I could have myself. The one thing we can agree on is that you could be in danger. We'll take it from there."

She nodded before telling him they needed to turn right on South Temple. He followed her directions until they passed Reservoir Park and entered the Federal Heights area where many of the ivy-covered mansions built by the mining magnates of old were elegantly preserved.

"Is Denise prepared to go along with our plan in order to spare her brother?"

"Yes. She said she'd follow our lead, then send Rod on an errand. That will give us enough time to talk in private."

"Good."

"Here's her house."

Roman pulled the car to a stop at the curb in front of a large, Italian renaissance-style home, then flashed her a probing glance. "From everything you've told me, Rod will be a difficult person to fool. Get ready to put on the greatest acting performance of your life. If we can convince him, then we're home free where anyone else is concerned."

She watched him reach in his trouser pocket and pull out a solitaire diamond ring. "I picked this up to make everything look real. Let's hope it isn't too big. Give me your left hand."

Brit's eyes grew huge as he slid the engagement ring onto her finger. To her surprise, it fit just fine. "Now we're official, but you look as if you could use a little shock treatment to get things going."

Before she realized it, he'd leaned across the seat and kissed her mouth. "That was for Rod's sake, in case he's watching.'' He kissed her again, applying more pressure. "You taste of strawberries.''

She drew away, hot-faced. A large blue-white stone sparkled up at her.

"Have you ever been in love, Brit?''

"There was one boy in high school, but like most first love relationships, it couldn't flourish because we were too young. I met another man in college. I liked him a lot, but not enough to marry. When I realized how serious he was getting, I broke it off.''

"Did you live together?''

"No.'' After a tension-filled silence she said, "I don't intend to sleep with any man until I'm married first.''

"You're a wise woman,'' came the deep-sounding rejoinder.

He slid his arm around her shoulders and they walked to the front porch of the oak-shaded, two-story mansion together. His solid strength felt good to her.

"I'm afraid moving in with me will raise some eyebrows.''

A blush swept over her face. "Yes.''

"We'll be 'married' in three days' time, which should circumvent any gossip. To outsiders, our marriage will look real.''

He held on to her and rang the bell, his nearness playing havoc with her emotions. Suddenly the door opened.

"*Brit!*''

She smiled at Denise's fourteen-year-old brother. "How are you doing, Rod? Can we come in?''

"Sure.''

They moved inside. Rod called to his sister that they had company.

"I'll be right there,'' came a shout from the rear of the house.

"Rod? This is Roman Lufka. Remember I told you that I had a really serious boyfriend in high school?''

"Yeah?'' His interested gaze was fixed on Roman.

"Well, it was Roman."

"That's right," Roman broke in, nestling her even closer to his body. "I had to move back east with my parents and then I went in the Marines. But I never forgot Brit, and decided to come back to Salt Lake to live. We've been talking since I returned. One thing led to another, and we're going to get married right away."

"That's great. Where are you going to live? I hope it's close to us."

"Afraid not, Rod. I bought a home in Olympus Cove. Do you know where that is?"

"Sure. Near the turnoff to Alta and Brighton. Do you ski?"

"It's my favorite sport," Roman asserted with a grin.

"Mine, too."

"When the snow flies, Brit and I will take you with us."

While Brit digested that amazing announcement, Rod's excited gaze darted to hers. "Brit doesn't ski."

Roman turned to her, a loving expression in his eyes which could have deceived anyone. "Then I'll have to teach you."

"I hope I'm included in that invitation," Denise chimed in, a pert brunette who breezed into the room wearing cut-offs and a blouse. Though she knew the gravity of the situation, she wore a sunny smile which almost deceived Brit.

"Hey, Sis— Did you know Brit's getting married?"

"She told me over the phone."

Denise gave Brit a hug, then shook Roman's hand. "I knew you were the important person in Brit's past. That's why no man has ever been able to get to first base with her. It's been a long time since high school, Roman." She winked one of her appealing brown eyes at him, then grabbed Brit's hand to inspect the ring at close range.

"It's absolutely breathtaking, Brit. You lucky..." she murmured under her breath.

Brit and Denise had been best friends since they were

ten years old, long enough for Brit to realize Denise had just sent her a private message.

Roman's mouth turned up at the corner. Obviously he was amused and pleased that Denise was playing her part so well.

"Denise—" Brit interjected at last "—since Roman is my fiancé, I want you two to become close friends."

"That won't be hard," Denise exclaimed. "Rod? I think we should celebrate. Why don't you run to the store and bring home some drinks and donuts. Dad left money in the drawer in the kitchen."

"Okay. I'll go."

"You have a nice brother," Roman said as soon as Rod disappeared out the front door. "In fact you did a masterful job of covering up the truth, Ms. Martin."

"Denise," she urged him before her expression grew solemn. "Thank you. So did you. I mean—you and Brit— Well, let's just say that you both could have fooled me."

"That's good."

"Please." She spread her hands. "Make yourselves comfortable. Rod will be back before we know it."

"I'm glad he's out of earshot. Just so you know, I've assigned some of my colleagues to keep round-the-clock surveillance on you and your brother. As I told Brit, no one knows how much information Baird picked up on the two of you that you're not aware of. We *do* know he mentioned you in the letters to Brit, so I'm not taking any chances."

"Thank you, Roman." Denise's voice shook. "Like Brit, my parents and I will be willing to pay any price for peace of mind."

"We'll worry about the bill later, all right?"

She nodded. "You're very kind. What can I do to help?"

"For one thing, we'll want you and Rod to witness our wedding in three days' time. I'm thinking we'll do it at Brit's parents' home, if they agree."

"Three days?" Denise blinked.

"That's right," he murmured. "We have to move fast."

Brit spoke up. "I—I'm sure it will be fine with Mom and Dad, Roman."

He nodded approvingly before his gaze switched back to Denise. "What we need from you is to throw us a party day after tomorrow. Let's make it an evening affair, informal. I'll pay for the pizza. Phone anyone you want. Brit's friends from work, from her church, your mutual friends."

"Like a couples' shower?"

"Exactly." He grinned. "You know the kind."

Denise's eyes looked mischievous. "I do."

"When we leave here, you can get on the phone to people. As for right now, I want you to tell me everything you can remember about Glen Baird from the very first moment you saw him. I want to hear any details you can share, no matter how insignificant they may have appeared to you at the time."

She shared a private look with Brit. "I'm sure she's told you everything. He gave all of us the creeps. But when everyone shied away from him, I felt kind of bad for him. That is until we got home and he started sending Brit those ghastly letters."

Roman nodded. "I can understand that. Most stalkers are disgruntled humans reaching out for love or attention in the only way they know how. In the course of their actions, they make mistakes a child could follow and are soon caught.

"The large percentage don't have intentions of causing physical injury, though they put their victims through unquestionable hell and emotional anguish. Unfortunately Baird is an unknown commodity, which is why we need to assume he could be dangerous to Brit and you."

Brit stirred restlessly. "I think being stalked is one of the most awful things that can be done to a person."

Roman's gaze flicked to her. "It's the reason for the anti-stalking laws. But in the end, it comes down to money. Our local law enforcement agencies don't have the funds to pay for extended stakeouts and surveillance.

"This last year I've been gathering information to prepare a bill for the Utah legislature which asks that public funds be granted to known stalking victims to bring their perpetrators to justice in the shortest amount of time possible. Bills like this are being initiated in other states, as well.

"But enough of that for now. You two need to help me understand Baird. Try to remember. Any little detail could help."

You're an amazing man, Roman Lufka. One in a million. How was I lucky enough to have picked you out of all the other private investigators?

CHAPTER THREE

"YOUR parents are delightful people, Brit."

In the darkness his deep voice reached out to touch her as they drove along Wasatch Boulevard toward his home. The thought of living with him filled her with an inexplicable excitement. Try as she might, she was having trouble remembering that he was simply a private investigator hired to guard her. On both an emotional and physical level, no man had ever affected her this profoundly.

"Thank you. They were very impressed with you, too." *So impressed, in fact, that they were willing to put their faith in his hands. Not once did they raise an eyebrow over the unorthodox situation.*

Brit wasn't surprised. Roman made a powerful impact on people. Even Denise hadn't been immune to his commanding, virile appeal.

As for her parents, their eagerness to comply with Roman's wishes and put on a wedding in so short a time—despite her father's heart condition—was nothing short of miraculous. They acted almost as if it were going to be the real thing, conversing animatedly with Roman, treating him like a true son-in-law to be.

The specter of Glen Baird seemed to have taken a back seat to the wedding preparations, all of which Roman assured them he would handle down to the last detail. Tonight Brit, herself, could be forgiven for thinking the unsolicited letters sent by that freak were a figment of her imagination.

"We're home," he murmured at last, slowing down to turn into the driveway of a home hidden by trees on densely wooded property. He pressed the Genie on his sun visor and they slid quietly into the double car garage where she saw a slate-blue BMW convertible parked.

The modern glass-and-wood house on Spruce Hollow Drive, aptly named for its many pine trees, was definitely a man's domain. No feminine frills anywhere, yet it invited.

When Roman came around to help her from the car, her arm accidentally brushed against his solid male chest, sending another dart of awareness through her body. On trembling legs she followed him through a door at the side of the garage into an entry hall where framed graphics of surrealistic drawings hung on the walls, capturing her attention.

Brit fell in love with the hardwood floors stained in a dark walnut color. The wood moldings and wainscoting against the off-white walls of the main living areas came as a surprise and added a traditional flavor. The same dark stained shutters at the windows gave total privacy, while the leather easy chairs and sofas, modern lighting and glass dining table off the kitchen with its own bar counter and stools gave the interior warmth.

A book-lined study complete with cherrywood desk and computer software, also contained a large television and VCR. Everything was tasteful, comfortable and unpretentious.

"The bedrooms are along this hallway. Mine is in front. I'll put you in the middle bedroom because it has a comfortable queen-size bed, and the bathroom is just across the hall. I've been using the last bedroom as a storeroom. It needs to be decorated and furnished. Unfortunately I haven't had the time to see about it yet."

Because of people like me, she mused guiltily.

He sounded very matter of fact, but Brit couldn't stop thinking about the sleeping arrangements. During the night, a mere wall would be separating them. Except for her father, she'd never lived in the same house with a man.

Sleeping in Roman's home would be a very different proposition. Somehow she was going to have to forget that his bed was so close to hers. But try as she might, she knew she wouldn't be able to prevent certain intimate pictures of him from forming in her mind.

His strong, whipcord frame and dark good looks made her think thoughts she'd never entertained about a man in relationship to herself. They brought the heat to her cheeks as he paused at the door to the middle bedroom.

She felt his narrowed gaze wander over her. No doubt he'd noticed her flushed face. "Make yourself at home. I've already done up your bed with fresh linen and put clean towels in the bathroom for you."

She swallowed hard, unable to meet his eyes. "Thank you again. It seems like that is all I ever say to you."

"It's nice to hear," came the low-pitched response. "Just remember. If you didn't need my services, I would be out of a job. I should be the one thanking you."

At that comment she couldn't help but smile, then shyly met his level gaze. It was a mistake. In the semidarkness of the hall, their proximity, combined with his masculinity, was all too potent. "Your point is well taken. Nevertheless, I am grateful."

She noted the quick rise and fall of his chest, wondering what exactly was going through *his* mind. After all, it was almost midnight.

Most likely he was anxious to do whatever it was he did when he was alone. Providing living quarters for a client who was going to be underfoot around the clock had to be a new experience for him, too. The last thing she wanted was to be a burden.

"I—I'm sure you're tired, Roman. I know I am, so I'll say good-night and see you in the morning."

She'd moved halfway into the room when he said, "Why don't you join me for a nightcap first?"

Much as she would have loved to say yes, she didn't dare. For a lot of reasons she was afraid to explore, it would be better if she went straight to bed. Besides, he'd only mentioned the idea out of courtesy to a guest. "I appreciate the offer, but I had a soda at Mom and Dad's."

His unreadable expression didn't change. "All right then. Sleep well." After hesitating a moment longer, he disappeared down the hall, leaving her feeling out of sorts.

Though her body was exhausted, she couldn't imagine being able to sleep. Maybe a hot shower would help her mind as well as her body to relax. Grabbing a nightgown and robe from her suitcase, she crossed the hall to the bright, modern bathroom and shut the door.

The fluffy towels, a black, beige and white stripe, reminded her of him, making it impossible for her to turn off her errant thoughts. The soap and shampoo he supplied, *everything* carried his stamp, increasing her cognizance of his vital, living presence in her life.

She slipped out of her clothes and submitted herself to the spray, wishing she could blot him from her consciousness. Eight hours ago she hadn't known of his existence.

How could one man have changed her life so drastically since four o'clock this afternoon?

Roman could hear the water running while he locked up the house and turned off lights. Much as he tried to concentrate on anything else, he couldn't prevent vivid images of the woman in the shower from passing through his mind.

He'd entertained houseguests on numerous occasions, mostly his brother and sister-in-law and their children.

This was different.

No way could he forget Brit Langford was standing under that water. With clothes on, she was breathtaking. The sight of her without—

Stop right there, Lufkilovich.

Realizing it was going to be a long night, he headed for the kitchen and pulled a can of beer from the fridge. He rarely drank anything alcoholic, but tonight he needed something to offset the adrenaline running rampant through his body.

When the beer didn't give him the relief he craved, he

had a strong urge to call his elder brother, Yuri. But it was two in the morning in New York. Out of the question!

He could phone his best friend, Cal Rawlings, Diana's husband. Unfortunately it was past their bedtime and he hated waking either of them.

The only other person he felt inclined to confide in was Chief Wilson. Nevada was an hour earlier than Salt Lake. Maybe it wouldn't be too late to give him a jingle and discuss Brit's case with him.

The older man reminded Roman of his deceased father. They'd hit it off during the stakeout. Crazy as it was, he wanted the chief and his wife to attend the mock wedding. Or maybe he just wanted verification that he'd done the right thing in going undercover as Brit's husband.

To his chagrin, when he made the phone call, there was no answer and no machine asking that he leave a message. It could mean the chief had gone to bed. Or he and his wife were out somewhere.

Frustrated, Roman turned off the kitchen light and headed for his ensuite bathroom to brush his teeth. He'd have to phone him in the morning.

All was quiet in the house. Brit had gone to bed. By the time he'd slid under the covers, he was angry with himself and glad he hadn't talked to anyone.

You're losing it, Lufkilovich. The woman asleep in the next room has slipped past all your reliable defenses and has somehow worked her way beneath your skin. You're not the same man you were before you took this case.

Far into the night Roman wrestled with his own particular demons, then shot out of bed when he heard a scream that sounded like the fabric of a blood-curdling nightmare.

Brit!

He entered her room without knocking and turned on the overhead light, forgetting that he wore nothing more than the bottom half of his sweats.

She was thrashing about under her covers, making terrified moaning sounds, obviously deeply disturbed.

Cursing the hairy-faced monster who had done this to her, he sat down on the side of the bed and called her name, urging her to wake up.

Her eyes suddenly flew open. Through the curtain of her disheveled hair, he could see they were glazed over. She didn't recognize him.

"Brit— It's Roman." He smoothed the ash-gold strands from her pale face. Right now she possessed an almost ethereal beauty. But it was the moisture on her cheeks that brought out his protective instincts like nothing he'd ever experienced in quite the same way before. "You've had a nightmare."

His voice appeared to bring her back to some semblance of reality. "I—I don't understand."

She was disoriented. "You're at my house, Brit. Remember? I heard you cry out."

She blinked before realizing the state of her undress and lifted the sheet to cover herself. During her struggle, the pale blue nylon gown she was wearing had become somewhat twisted, the sleeve having fallen down her arm to the elbow. He'd seen enough to guarantee that he'd never get to sleep now. Maybe never again.

A deep rose color tinted her dewy skin.

She knew what he'd seen. Lord.

"I'm all right now," she whispered, averting her eyes.

The hardest thing he'd ever had to do was get up from that bed. Looming over her, he said, "I'm sorry to have burst in on you like that, but the terror in your voice wouldn't let me ignore you."

She shook her head. "I-it's all right, Roman. I'm sorry that I disturbed you. Since those letters started coming, I've had a lot of violent dreams. Living alone, I guess I didn't realize just how bad they've become."

"Can I bring you some tea, or some hot chocolate? Something to soothe your nerves?"

She moistened her lips. "No, thank you. I'll be all right. I brought some books with me. Reading always helps."

"You're sure? If you want, I'll stay with you awhile."

"No," she said a little too forcefully for his liking. "I've imposed on you enough. Please—go back to bed. I'll be fine."

He sucked in his breath, fighting the almost overwhelming desire to climb under the covers and hold her so she wouldn't be frightened anymore.

"If you need me during the night, call out and I'll hear you."

Slowly she lifted her gaze to his, those orbs so dark with turbulent emotion, they looked closer to black than blue. "I pray I won't disturb you again."

"I don't mind," came the words from deep inside him.

Her eyes closed. "But I do. Good night, Roman."

He turned on the bedside lamp. "Good night."

As soon as he'd flicked off the overhead light and shut the door, she reached for the novel she'd put on the nightstand. Twenty minutes later, after she'd read the same page for the tenth time, she gave up, turned out the light and sank down under the covers.

Her body felt alive in a brand new way, like it was on fire...

When he'd looked at her just now, something had ignited in the recesses of his eyes, turning the flecks in those green irises to gold. It was as if a charge of electricity had leaped clear of his body to find a place in her own, energizing her with his life-giving force.

Though he hadn't touched any part of her except her hair, she felt a connection with him as real and vital as something tangible. Filled with more intimate thoughts of him, her eyelids finally drooped and at some point she knew no more until she heard him call her to breakfast.

Through bleary eyes she glanced at her watch. It was ten to nine. She never slept in this late, but after the events of last night, Brit realized her body needed the extra sleep. Still, she was embarrassed by what had transpired. Furthermore she felt selfish, especially when she'd kept

Roman awake part of the night and knew there was a huge amount of work to be accomplished today.

After scrambling to make her bed, she freshened up, then dressed in jeans and a blouse to join him.

Cereal, eggs, juice awaited her at the dining room table. She tucked right in and told him food had never tasted so good before. Fortunately she caught herself before she blurted that *he* looked good, too. Especially in that black T-shirt and hip-hugging Levi's.

Last night all he'd been wearing were the bottom half of his pajamas or some facsimile. He was a gorgeous male. She could hardly breathe just remembering the sight of him when she'd first been awakened by his voice.

With difficulty, she finished eating, then took her plate to the sink. "Let me do the dishes, please."

His enticing mouth curved upward. "That's what I was hoping to hear, but they'll have to wait. I've phoned a moving company. They're sending a small van to your condo within forty-five minutes. We need to get over there right now so you can pack what you need to bring here. The rest we'll put in storage."

"I won't want much."

He studied her for a brief moment. "Bring anything you like. There's plenty of room."

"Even for Tiger?"

"*Tiger?*"

"She's an alley cat who comes around once in a while for food and a little love."

A smile hovered at the corner of his mouth. "If she's there, bring her along, too."

"I didn't mean it, Roman. She's a wild cat and knows how to survive. But thank you anyway," she said softly, rubbing her palms together before looking away.

So far there was nothing about Roman Lufka she didn't like. She'd been trying to find something—anything—which would help her keep her perspective in this situation.

"I've already arranged for your phone and fuel to be

disconnected. The post office now has a hold on your mail. We'll pick it up every day at the Foothill outlet. In case this weirdo changes his mind and sends you something else in the mail, I want the postmaster to open it. That kind of corroborating testimony will weigh heavily, if and when charges are brought against him.''

She experienced relief knowing she would never have to open a letter or package from Glen Baird again.

"Roman— I—I realize I sound like a broken record, but I don't know how to thank you.''

"It's my job, Brit.''

"One that puts your life in danger all the time.''

"Not all the time,'' he insisted wryly. "If you want to know the truth, it was inevitable that I was born with a desire to live life on the edge.''

She blinked. "Inevitable?''

"Hmm… Perhaps you've heard of C and G Surveillance Products, Inc.?''

"No. I presume you're talking about bugging devices and the like.''

"That's right. My grandfather, Constantine, and his brother, Gregorio, started the business before WWII broke out. Later, when the military came to them with a contract, the company grew into an enormous enterprise which my father and uncles expanded. By the time my brother Yuri and I, and all our cousins came along, it had gone national with outlets all over the country.''

Brit was fascinated. "You mean your company makes suitcases that blow apart like we see in the James Bond movies?''

He smiled. "Can you imagine what heaven that was? Two little boys growing up, playing with every spy gadget and camera known to mankind?''

"I can. It's something which would have appealed to me, as well. For a period of time in my young life, I wanted to be a boy because they had more fun. That is until Lance Crawford, the marble king of the fifth grade, told me I was a better player than all the boys, and gave me his favorite steelie marble. From that point on, I was kind of glad to be a female.''

His chuckle joined hers and they stared at each other, fully enjoying the moment.

"By the time we were adults,'' he finally continued, "Yuri wanted to keep inventing stuff.''

"Like what, for instance?''

"Have you got all day?'' Roman quipped. "The truth is, there's every kind of camera known to man out there, and some you haven't even thought of. If you're really interested, I've got brochures. You're welcome to devour the contents.''

She gave him the benefit of an unguarded smile. "So he invents, and you try everything out.''

His lips quirked. "That's right. Today my brother is the CEO of the company. I'm a major stockholder, but I have my own life and I'm very content as I am. So you see? There's nothing noble about what I do for a living.

"Don't imbue me with honorable traits for which I can claim no ownership. Basically I'm very selfish. Otherwise I'd be back in New York with the family, helping my brother and cousins in the family business. You might call me the black sheep.''

Brit detected undertones and found herself wanting to know more about him. He'd talked about his family, but what about the woman in his life? Surely no man like Roman Lufka would be without one. In fact, she imagined there wasn't a female alive who wouldn't be susceptible to his charisma.

Had an ex-wife or a fiancée been the reason he'd left the East Coast and his family to move to Salt Lake?

Clearing her throat, Brit said, "If you mean that the other aspects of your life have to be put on hold while you're undercover, then I suppose anyone waiting for a relationship with you would be frustrated.''

His eyes narrowed on her mouth. "That's one way of putting it," he murmured cryptically, sounding far away.

"Well, whatever it's worth—" her voice trembled "—you're a rare breed of man. All I can do is thank heaven that there are people like you, willing to lay down your life for a fellow human being."

He put his hands on his hips. She swallowed hard at the attractive male standing before her.

"I appreciate your well-meant expression of gratitude, Brit. It has been duly noted. Now let's agree to get off the subject and head for your condo."

She nodded, but it was hard to put a rein on her emotions.

"We'll have the movers clear everything out, then turn your keys in to the landlord. Shall we go?"

As they moved down the hallway to the door leading to the garage, Roman grabbed a duffel bag sitting on a chair.

"What's in that?" she inquired after they'd gotten in his car and he'd pressed the remote to open the garage door.

"A few gadgets I'm going to install at your condo while it remains vacant. If Baird attempts to break in, we'll have it all on film."

When that revelation had gotten through to her, Brit's gaze swerved to his face, but all she could see was his arresting profile. "I bet your house is full of them, isn't it?"

Except for the rev of the engine, there was silence.

"Roman?" she prodded when he didn't say anything.

He finally spoke. "As you well know, last night you cried loud enough for me to hear you without the aid of anything electronic." He read her mind with astonishing ease. "I'm not surprised. Hopefully you'll start to feel safe with me and sleep without being disturbed by nightmares."

Guilt consumed her once more. "I'm sorry."

"Don't say that again," he warned. "If it will make you feel any better, I was working on your case."

He backed the car out of the driveway and they were off.

"If that's true, then when do you sleep?"

"When I need to. Don't you worry about it."

She took a fortifying breath. "You really think Glen's coming soon, don't you?"

"Yes."

"I know you're running on instinct, but I have a feeling there's a little more to it than that. Please tell me. I can take the truth a lot better than I can handle just sitting here agonizing over what it is you're holding back from me."

"All right," he muttered. "A colleague in the New York City Police Department has been doing some digging for me. I received his fax at three this morning. It verified what Glen Baird wrote in his first letter to you, that he preferred to call you Brittany, because it was a French name, and he'd spent time in the province of Brittany.

"It seems that a Glen Baird, then from Indiana, took a package tour of Spain, North Africa and France, with Voyager Tours in the summer of 1992. Brittany was on the itinerary."

Brit! You wanted the truth. So why are you dreading what he's about to tell you?

"In the fall of 1994, while he was living in Tennessee, he took another tour to South America with Sunburst Tours. As far back as 1989, while he was living in Oklahoma, he took a trip to the California coast, always with a different group tour company."

"He's lived all those places?" Brit cried out.

"That's right. Each time he's held a different job. Sometimes with the railroad, other times with a trucking company or a manufacturing plant."

She turned anxiously in his direction. "So what are you thinking?"

There was a slight hesitation before he said, "I have a hunch he goes on these tours to find women. Obviously he's never been successful, which might account for the large number of times he has changed jobs and moved on. It also makes me wonder if he has a record of harassment dating back as far as the time when he first came to Salt Lake. My sources are researching that now."

"It makes me sick."

"*He's* sick. That's why I'm not taking any chances where you're concerned. I plan to investigate every possibility," he ground out fiercely. "Now maybe you can understand why I wanted to move fast on this one. He's already left Madison, and an APB hasn't turned up anything on him yet. It's vital we set the trap now, just in case. If you can, leave the worrying to me, all right?"

She nodded, but his suspicions left her brooding. It was just as well they had work to do helping the movers, otherwise she would have made herself sick over the latest revelations.

After everything had been cleared out and they'd gone to talk to the landlord, she thought Roman would take her back to the house so he could leave for work. When she said as much to him, he stared at her with a puzzled expression.

"You *are* my work."

The truth of his words finally sank in.

After they'd gotten in the car he murmured, "Where shall we go to get your wedding dress?"

Her heart leaped in her chest. "You mean, now?"

"Of course. We also have to see about the cake, the food, the flowers. I need to arrange for a tuxedo and a pianist who will provide traditional background music for us."

Under ordinary circumstances it was understood that the bride took care of all the wedding preparations. The groom was supposed to be the reluctant one who didn't show up until the moment when he had to say, "I do."

With Roman ticking off the list of things to be done before the big day arrived, Brit felt superfluous.

Be honest, Brit. You're hurting like crazy because this

isn't a real wedding. Because you're not really marrying Roman Lufka.

You can't ever let him see how all this is affecting you on the inside.

"I suppose we could go to one of the department stores downtown for my dress. There's a tuxedo rental on South Temple. We could stop there on the way."

"I know the exact place. Let's go."

Within fifteen minutes they'd reached the shop she had in mind. It didn't take Roman long to pick out several styles and colors of tuxedos, all of which made him look incredibly handsome. With a legitimate reason to stare, she drank her fill of his tall, dark figure.

But one glance at him in black with a silver cummerbund and Brit couldn't prevent herself from voicing her preference with such enthusiasm, the college-age man waiting on them grinned from ear to ear.

Roman couldn't have helped but pick up on the rush of emotion that accompanied her outburst, but he kept his thoughts well hidden.

Furious with herself, she remained silent while he made arrangements to pick up his tuxedo on the morning of the wedding. When that was accomplished, they headed for town. If Roman wondered why she was so quiet, he didn't say anything. *Thank heaven.*

The bridal department at Z.C.M.I. had every kind of wedding dress the modern bride could hope to find. But to her shock, Roman seemed dissatisfied with what he saw.

"I believe there's an exclusive bridal shop on Third South. Let's go there," he muttered, not bothering to ask her opinion.

Brit knew the one. It was a boutique that carried a lot of internationally renown designer fashions. A shop for the wealthy.

"I don't understand—" she said as they got back in the car and drove the short distance to the other store.

"None of those dresses looked like you," came the even-toned explanation, turning her insides to liquid. "I'll know the one I like, just as you knew the jacket you liked the second I shrugged into that black tux."

She *had* given herself away earlier. Roman's eyes and antennae missed nothing!

"Do you have a dress along simple lines—no extra frills—something that looks demure, like a maiden?" she heard Roman ask the salesclerk a few minutes later, after they'd entered Celeste's Bridal Boutique.

A maiden? Brit mouthed the words in stunned surprise. *Because he saw her as young and virginal?*

The stylish older woman perused Brit's face and figure. If she thought it strange that the groom was actually buying the wedding dress for his bride, she didn't show it and Brit supposed that more and more the tradition of the groom not seeing the bride's gown before the big day was being overlooked.

Suddenly the clerk nodded. "I know just the gown. It's been waiting for you! Come." She motioned.

Brit had no choice but to follow her to the fitting room, leaving Roman behind with a glimmer of satisfaction hovering around his mouth.

"That incredible fiancé of yours has exquisite taste," she commented moments later, carrying an impossibly white wedding dress in a soft crepe-like material over her arm. "You're a lucky young woman. The creation is a Rimini original. The Italians know exactly how to drape a woman. This is from a private showing of the famed 'Madonna of the Pieta' collection."

While she spoke, Brit took off her clothes, donned the underslip and allowed the woman to help ease the dress over her head.

When she could breathe again, she looked in the mirror and gasped in disbelief. The gown was so simple, it put her in mind of a painting she'd seen in France of a long garment worn by Joan of Arc. The simple round neck and sleeves to the wrist gave the slim dress which fell to the floor a demure look of purity and virtue.

"Here is the *pièce de résistance*." So saying, the clerk placed a floor-length mantilla over Brit's head. Made of the finest sheer tulle, the two-inch border of French Alençon lace framed her face and fell to the carpet, creating the illusion of a madonna.

"It's perfect," she heard a deep, familiar male voice whisper. "We'll take it."

Still looking in the mirror, her shocked blue eyes met Roman's. The way he was staring at her, the sudden stillness of his hard, lean body set hers trembling. She had this suffocating feeling in her chest.

The second the clerk had gone, Brit turned a flushed face to Roman whose gaze roamed freely over her figure. "This dress is going to cost a small fortune."

"Let me worry about that."

Her rounded chin lifted in defiance. "It's beyond my price range." But in truth, she adored it. This was the dress she would want if they were really getting married. To wear it to a mock ceremony would be sacrilege.

After a tension-filled pause, "Just so you understand, I'm a very rich man and can afford it," he fired back, his irritation pronounced.

From all he'd told her, she suspected he came from a monied background, but the bald revelation caught her on the raw. "Unfortunately, *I* can't. Since I hired you, we'll have to function on *my* meager budget."

"I'm in agreement with that *except* where this dress is concerned. As the clerk said, it was made for you, and it's the one I want. Let it be my wedding gift to you. You can save it for the day when you give yourself to your true husband."

As the electricity crackled between them, she felt a strange twinge of pain in the region of her heart. Somehow she couldn't imagine anyone else but the magnificent man standing before her filling the role of her lawfully wedded husband. Not even if she lived to be a hundred.

She swallowed hard. "No, Roman."

"It's already decided," he said in a tone of steely command. "Now, if you'll turn around, I'll undo you and save the clerk the trouble. We're in a hurry."

CHAPTER FOUR

MUCH as Roman could tell Brit wanted to scream her protest, he could count on her not to make a scene in front of the salesclerk who was innocent of the whole affair.

Like a robot, Brit removed the mantilla and clutched it to her bosom before doing his bidding. She trembled when his hands went to the satin-covered buttons, slowly undoing each eyelet. As he made his way down her back to her waist, his fingertips savored the velvety smoothness of her skin till they met the barrier of her slip, a thin tissue-like substance which trapped her warmth.

The perfume emanating from her reached out to him like a living thing. His breath caught in his throat as the insane impulse to remove her dress and everything else that hid her body from his hungry gaze virtually overwhelmed him.

He had no business being this close to her, no business finding any excuse he could conjure to go on touching her.

What in the hell do you think you're doing in a ladies' fitting room, undressing the woman you've been hired to protect, Lufkilovich?

Dear God— Another minute and Brit was going to need protection from *him!* Visions of what had occurred in the middle of the night didn't help the situation. His plan to go undercover as her husband was backfiring at a breathtaking pace.

In a burst of self-deprecation, he removed his hands as if her skin had scorched him. ''I'll wait for you at the desk,'' he muttered to the back of her head. The desire to tangle his hands in the ash-blond hair that swirled in attractive disarray across her bare shoulders was palpable. He

53

needed to get out of there before he did something unforgivable.

"I—I'll hurry and change," came the slightly muffled response, causing him to wonder if his nearness was affecting her the same way.

Before leaving the room he added, "Since it doesn't need any alterations, I'll inform the clerk we're taking the dress with us."

Without giving her a chance to respond, he left her to her own devices, breathing deeply to quell the violent hammering of his heart.

After telling the saleswoman to put the charge on his credit card, he pulled the phone from his pocket and called Cal.

Early that morning he'd had a long talk with his friend about Brit's case. They'd ended the conversation by tentatively planning a special dinner out for that evening. To make everything look more real, he wanted to show Brit off in a public place, a sort of informal engagement dinner with champagne and dancing.

Since Brit had already talked with Diana over the phone and had made a personal connection, the four of them ought to enjoy each other's company. Now was his chance to finalize their plans.

Sooner than he would have believed, Brit reappeared ready to go. The clerk thanked them both with a smile and handed the garment bag to Roman. After they left the shop, his companion remained curiously taciturn on their walk to the car.

"Do you know of a good pastry shop?" he questioned after he'd spread the bag across the back seat and started the ignition.

"Yes. Becker's. Their wedding cakes are famous. It's on South Temple, a few blocks away from the tuxedo place. The Becker family are close friends of our family.

"He escaped from Germany with his mother when he was just a young boy. They'd witnessed the shooting of a group of Jews behind their pastry shop and decided to get out. His mother sewed money in the lining of his little coat. They fled the country by holding on to the underneath of a boxcar of a train.'' Her voice trembled.

Roman was listening intently. Everything Brit did or said captured his imagination, making him want to know more. For the life of him he couldn't comprehend what his world had been like before she'd entered it.

Forget your fantasies, Lufkilovich. You're not free to dream. Remember? Something else owns you, body and soul.

''Remind me to tell you about my grandparents' escape from Russia. The tales sound incredibly similar.''

''I'd love to hear it,'' she enthused. There was an earnestness, a sincerity about her that was gnawing away at all his good intentions to remain aloof and professional.

To his surprise, the famous Mr. Becker happened to be in the back of the store. When he learned Brit was in front with her fiancé, he came out dressed in a white shirt and trousers to shake hands with her and Roman.

The congenial, soft-spoken gentleman spent a good half hour with them. After promising to create a special cake as his wedding present to them, he spent the rest of the time exchanging refugee stories with Roman.

When it surfaced that the Beckers also lived in Federal Heights, Roman invited him and his family to attend their wedding. This brought a silent message of approval from Brit whose lustrous blue eyes unexpectedly smiled up at him.

Roman discovered that he'd like to witness that phenomenon on a permanent basis. *Impossible*, a voice nagged at him.

Disturbed by the recurring trend of his thoughts, he thanked Mr. Becker, then ushered Brit from the store.

''I'm hungry.''

''I am, too,'' she agreed.

''Let's stop for a hamburger before we see about the

flowers. Then I suggest we go home and rest up for the evening ahead.''

His remark caused her eyes to widen. ''What do you mean?''

Lord, she had an exquisite mouth. Last night he'd only had a brief taste of those untutored lips. Heaven help him, *he yearned for more.*

''Diana, the woman on the phone at my office, is the wife of my best friend, Cal Rawlings. They're taking us out for an engagement dinner.''

She shook her head, then turned away. ''I—I don't think we need to go that far.'' Her voice trailed.

Before he'd said the words, Roman knew his plan would meet with objections, but he was ready for her. ''It's important that we carry out this charade. Anything less convincing will defeat our plans. I don't need to remind you that it may be some time before Baird shows up, *if* he shows at all.''

The sudden quiet coming from her side of the car pleased him.

''We have to behave exactly the way we would if you were truly my fiancée, Brit. Believe me, if this wedding were real, Cal would insist on a celebration dinner.'' *So would Yuri and Jeannie.*

The thought of his brother reminded him that before too much more time passed, he needed to phone Yuri and explain that one of his clients was staying at his house for an indefinite period.

If Yuri should happen to call and hear Brit's voice, he might falsely assume that Roman was living with a woman and keeping it a secret. It would ruin Roman's cover as the heartbroken bachelor of the Lufkilovich family, a cover which had served him well over the years that he'd been a member of the CIA.

It would also hurt Yuri and Jeannie in an intensely personal way which Roman had no desire to contemplate. His elder brother was Roman's idol. He'd always looked up to him and loved him. The fact that Roman had been forced to keep his CIA status a secret from Yuri had been the one constant source of pain in Roman's life.

He couldn't imagine doing that to a wife and children, thus the reason he'd made the decision early on to live out the rest of his earthly days alone.

Without conscious thought, he cast a covert glance at the hauntingly lovely female at his side. To live a lie with a sensitive woman like Brit Langford, to place her life and the lives of their children in danger, would be unconscionable. He could never do it.

What shocked him was that he could even envision the possibility of being married to her. *How long had he known her*? *Twenty-four hours*? He groaned to realize that no woman had ever impacted on his life to this extreme.

Whatever had possessed him to decide to play her husband?

He'd given Brit perfectly good reasons she could live with. Oddly enough, those same reasons didn't quite meet his own relentless scrutiny, filling him with alarm and confusion.

To his consternation, those same emotions seemed to intensify later that Saturday night when he escorted the object of his torment to the roof garden of the exclusive Empire Hotel in the heart of the city.

She looked a vision in a modest gray-blue silk sheath, her hair caught back in a French twist, reminding him of a young Grace Kelly, the famous blond American movie star of the fifties who ended up marrying a prince in real life.

Every eye, male or female, followed her movements as they walked through the ornate lobby to take the elevator. When they emerged on the top floor of the hotel overlooking the skyline, Roman immediately spied Cal whose jaw dropped open at the sight of Brit on Roman's arm. Diana, as well, looked taken aback, but she had the presence of mind to recover in time to nudge her husband so he wouldn't embarrass Roman or his female client.

"Brit?" Roman murmured a second later, his hand tightening on her elbow. "Allow me to introduce my dearest friends, Diana and Cal."

"How do you do?" Brit said with an engaging smile proffered at both of them. "I've especially looked forward to meeting you, Diana."

"Really?" she questioned in puzzlement. "Why?"

"Yesterday I was so frightened, you'll never know how grateful I was when you said you'd talk to one of the investigators about my case. You represented a lifeline to me. I can never thank you enough."

"What have I told you, Diana?" Roman interjected suavely. "Don't ever underestimate the part you play at the office."

"Thank you," she answered, sounding pleased.

Cal couldn't seem to take his eyes off Brit, not even when the *maître d'* guided them to their table at the window.

While they were given menus, Roman could read his friend's mind and almost dreaded the time when they would find themselves alone to talk in private. Cal would require a ruthless debriefing, something Roman wasn't up to. Not yet...

Uninterested for the moment in food, Roman found his escort infinitely more desirable. In the candlelight the periwinkle stones of her earrings sparkled with every heartbeat. But they couldn't match the brilliance of her eyes as she occasionally looked his way in polite response to a comment he'd purposely made to garner her attention. He'd love to know what was going on inside that beautiful head of hers.

The Roof had one of the better bands around. When they came out to play, Roman expelled the breath he'd been holding and rose to his feet. The need to feel Brit in his arms had grown into a permanent ache that required assuagement or he wasn't going to make it through dinner.

He didn't care if she wanted to dance or not. Without

giving her a choice, he pulled her chair away from the table, forcing her to join him. The heavy-handed gesture drew surprised glances from everyone, especially Brit, but Roman would worry about it later.

The only reality was the unfamiliar lethargy of his body which screamed with needs it seemed only this woman could satisfy.

But as they moved slowly around the floor, he sensed she was fighting him. Instead of melting against him, she held herself apart, whether out of fear or self-preservation, or both, he couldn't tell.

What he did know deep in his gut was that the desire he was feeling, was a mutual thing shared by both of them. Otherwise he wouldn't be able to detect the tiny pulse at her temple throbbing against his cheek, nor would her breathing be this shallow.

If he moved his hands the slightest bit, her body quivered in reaction. It took every bit of fortitude not to crush her against him until they melded as one flesh.

"Mind if I break in, old buddy?" Cal inquired seemingly out of nowhere. Roman detected a certain edge to his tone. "My wife needs to talk shop with you for a minute, and I haven't yet had the opportunity to dance with your client."

Roman steeled himself not to react. He knew exactly what Cal was doing, and why. Later he'd probably thank his friend for stepping in before any more damage was done, but right now he could easily plant a fist in that firm jaw.

With the greatest of reluctance he let Brit go. For an unguarded moment she looked as dazed as he felt before he relinquished her to Cal's care. If he didn't know his friend was madly in love with Diana, Roman wouldn't have yielded Brit at all, not even in the name of civility.

After he'd walked back to the table to pour himself another glass of champagne, Diana wisely remained silent. But the expression on her face was eloquent with meaning.

Feeling guiltier than hell, Roman drained it to the last

drop hoping to experience a numbing effect, then put down the glass so hard he heard the stem crack. This brought a shocked glance from Diana.

"Are you all right, Roman?"

He eyed her shrewdly. "You know damn well I'm not."

"She *is* lovely." Diana was probably better than anyone besides Yuri at reading his innermost thoughts.

"She's my *client*," he bit out in self-abnegation.

Diana's mouth curved upward. "But she's a woman first, and you're a man before you're a P.I. Can't you forgive yourself and enjoy the moment for what it is without getting wrapped up in all those noble ideals that rule your life and deprive you of what the rest of us take for granted?"

You've come closer to the truth than you realize, Diana, and I'd do just that if were a mere P.I., but I'm not.

There was no time for a reply, not even if Roman had manufactured one, because Cal and Brit had left the dance floor and were almost upon them.

Diana suddenly got up from the table. "Would you like to go to the powder room with me, Brit?"

"I was just going to ask you the same thing," came the quiet reply.

Roman grimaced, not knowing whether to be relieved or frustrated at the prospect of being left alone with Cal who never let anything go without a thorough dissection of the problem first.

Cal's eyes resembled slits as he sat back in the chair and stared Roman down. "How long *exactly* have you known this woman?"

"You already know the answer to that." His voice grated.

"Whoa." Cal broke out in a secret smile. "I always knew when it hit, you wouldn't know which way was up."

"Enjoying the show?" Roman fired back with uncharacteristic sarcasm.

Cal's smile widened into a grin. "What makes this so

nice is that Brit appears equally dazed and breathless in your presence.''

Try as he might, Roman couldn't tamp down the excitement that little piece of unsolicited information produced. Not when it came from someone who was as shrewd a judge of character and as close to him as Cal.

"You think it's *nice*?" Roman ground out, feeling uncontrollably aggressive and damn well close to exploding.

"All you've got is prewedding nerves. Only two more days, old son, and you're home free."

That did it. "Maybe your hearing is going out on you, *old son*," Roman retorted. "For the record, it's going to be a fake ceremony."

Cal didn't bat an eye. "Surely you're not going to let a little piece of legality stand in the way of performing your husbandly duty."

"Shut up, Cal."

"If *that's* what is bothering you," he went on talking unabashedly, "I know a *real* minister who would be more than happy to oblige."

"We're back, in case either of you wanted to know."

As far as Roman was concerned, Diana's melodic voice had intruded at precisely the right moment. He pushed himself away from the table and got out of the chair.

"That's good because something has come up and we've got to go." He purposely refrained from looking at Cal, and instead flashed a glance at Brit who appeared to be busy studying the napkin he'd just thrown down on the table next to the empty champagne glass. She'd barely touched hers.

Brit unexpectedly excused herself and headed for the elevator. Roman went after her, leaving Cal and Diana behind.

As soon as the doors closed he said, "Next time, wait for me to escort you, Brit. We're supposed to be engaged. Just now you forgot that fact."

She tossed her head impatiently. "I didn't forget. But

when you brought up the subject of leaving so abruptly, I assumed an emergency had arisen to do with your work. I was only trying to expedite matters.''

You idiot, Lufkilovich. ''I appreciate your sensitivity. This is a new role for both of us. Plan to stay close to me and follow my lead at the shower tomorrow night, then there will be no problem.''

''Speaking of tomorrow,'' she said as they got in his car a few minutes later, ''I really should put in a few hours at work. Usually on Sunday no one else will be there and I can get a lot accomplished without the phones ringing.''

''Fine. I'll come with you.''

She bowed her head. ''Is that really necessary? I mean, a security guard is always on duty. I hate to take you from your work.''

Roman was beginning to wonder if he and Cal had misread the signs and the attraction was all on Roman's side after all. It might save the day if that were the case.

But the very real possibility that her emotions *weren't* as involved as his, upset him a lot more than he would have imagined. He actually felt savage.

''We've already established that you hired me to work for you.''

''Then I won't go into the office.''

His brows formed a frown line. ''Surely your work is as important as mine.''

''It is, but I'd be dragging you away from your study where you can get a lot of other things done at the same time you're guarding me!'' she explained a little too hotly. *Good.* She wasn't as in control as he'd thought.

''That's true. Perhaps if this case takes longer than I originally anticipated, we can negotiate some sort of compromise.''

''You mean like my bringing home some of my work?''

''Exactly.'' For reasons he couldn't analyze right now, her suggestion went a long way toward appeasing him. ''It would be no trouble to get you a drafting table and equip the spare bedroom into an office for you. Let's just wait and see what develops. As for tomorrow, I go where you go.''

It took her a long time before she said, "All right." Her voice was practically inaudible. In the short time he'd known her, he had already learned that when she temporarily ran out of fight, she went very quiet. *He liked that aspect of her. Hell.* He liked *every* aspect of her.

So did half a dozen other guys he didn't know who had been invited to the party Denise gave for them the following evening. Married or single, they congregated around her, lit up when she talked, watched her as she moved easily around Denise's living room with Roman on her arm.

The simple, modest, black sleeveless dress provided the perfect foil for her gleaming ash-blond hair. It was an experience just to watch her walk, particularly when she was unconscious of her impact on the opposite sex.

To make things look normal, a couple of the P.I.s who were off duty came to the party with escorts. They introduced themselves as old friends of Roman's to go along with the story he'd told Denise's brother that he'd once lived in Salt Lake, before his parents moved to New York.

Before the party broke up, Denise asked for everyone's attention so they could play a game. Unbeknownst to him and Brit, everyone was supposed to have brought a gift that had some significance in their past lives. It could be anything, old or new.

The game started with the gifts for Brit first. As each was unwrapped, she had to recall the private memory which inevitably produced laughter and tears—an old record danced to, a class picture of an embarrassing moment, some castanets from a spring break trip to Mexico. Items that made Brit laugh and cry.

As Roman sat at her side, entranced, reacting the way any enamored fiancé would do, it suddenly occurred to him that he'd forgotten this party was all part of a charade. For a little while the lines had become so blurred that Roman himself hadn't been able to distinguish between truth and fiction. These people assumed his impending marriage to Brit was for real.

It felt far too real.

With this realization came a fresh wave of guilt over what he'd done. He'd told her that she would have to agree to his plan—which was to go undercover as her husband—or else find herself another P.I.

How glibly he'd told her that once her case was solved, she could go back to her normal life and announce to all her friends that their marriage hadn't been for real, that everything had been pretense.

He looked around the room at each animated face. Everyone here was happy for Brit. How were they going to feel when they found out the truth?

You've worked for the CIA too long.

After so many years of manufacturing one lie after another, Roman realized how easily he'd fabricated this plot to trap Glen Baird at his own game, never counting the cost to Brit and her friends. Until now, he'd always felt like what he'd done in the name of truth and justice was honorable.

"It's your turn, Roman," Denise prompted him, jerking him from his torturous thoughts. "I believe Eric—is it?—has a little something for you."

The first P.I. Roman had hired, *and* the greatest practical joker of all time, tossed him a package from the couch where he was sitting. A distinct twinkle in his eye warned Roman that he probably wouldn't like what was in the small, gaily wrapped box.

Roman felt Brit's watchful gaze on him as he undid the paper and lifted the lid, careful to make sure not even she could see inside.

A lily.

Under the right circumstances it might have been amusing, even funny, but Roman had never felt less like laughing. A new sickness hit him in the pit of his stomach.

Looking out at no one in particular, he quipped, "I'm afraid this one is censored for the time being." Acting on pure instinct, he pulled Brit close and whispered in her ear, "I'll tell you later." Then, to everyone's obvious delight, he gave her a resounding kiss on the mouth.

She blushed on cue and this produced the usual hoots and hollers from the crowd. His secrecy over the gift was a huge success so that everyone was grinning and speculating, making the usual groom innuendos.

Cal's gift saved the day. An expired ski pass to Snowbird, which brought up the subject of his favorite sport. At that point everyone started talking about the Winter Olympics coming to Utah. Much later on, the party broke up.

But Brit hadn't forgotten Eric's gift. The second they were in his car for the ride home she said, "May I see the box?"

"I'm not sure where I put it."

"It's in your suit pocket."

"It's private."

"I'm not a child."

No, you're not.

"Brit—I don't like spoiling a wonderful evening. Your friends are very nice."

"So are the P.I.s you invited."

"Then let's allow you to keep that opinion."

"You mean what Eric gave you could change it?"

"Maybe."

"I don't like lies, Roman."

His hands gripped the wheel so hard, his knuckles turned white.

Quicker than he would have believed, she leaned closer and reached inside his pocket. Since she was determined, Roman didn't try to stop her.

"Is this some kind of indecent *toy* I've never heard of?" she asked in a playful tone.

She's giving you a chance, Lufka.

"No. I wish it were," he muttered gruffly.

Out of the periphery he saw her take off the lid. Then he heard the inevitable gasp.

CHAPTER FIVE

"...AND now I pronounce you husband and wife. Roman, you may kiss your bride."

Though Phil, one of the P.I.s, had performed his part brilliantly as their minister, once again Roman had a hard time remembering the ceremony wasn't for real when he covered her mouth with his own. After last night's kiss, he wasn't surprised he didn't have to do all the work. She was learning to trust him. That's why he felt her lips respond with surprising warmth.

Unlike that first night in front of Denise's home, when he could have been forgiven for thinking he was kissing a piece of petrified wood, the bride he held in his arms was enticingly pliable.

He'd warned Brit that the wedding ceremony needed to look convincing, particularly when longtime friends of their family, people from her work and church were in attendance.

She hadn't disappointed him. Pleased she was such a fast learner, he unconsciously found himself deepening their kiss as he'd been aching to do. But it was a mistake. He'd known it would be, but it was too late for regrets as a fresh jolt of desire quickened his body.

Angry with himself, he took a steadying breath to relax, then lifted his mouth from hers, noting the stain on her cheeks. He shouldn't have enjoyed it so much with every eye on them. She wasn't that inexperienced that she didn't know what had just happened.

Cal's shrewd gaze locked with Roman's over her veil. He'd seen it, too. "May I be the first to congratulate the beautiful bride?'' Roman heard his good friend murmur a second later, helping to diffuse an uncomfortable moment.

What made everything so much worse was that when Cal got him alone, he would never let Roman hear the end of it. Neither would Phil.

"You look radiant," Diana enthused with a sincerity that didn't sound in the least feigned. She clung to Cal.

Diana had spoken the truth. Brit *glowed.*

Again Roman experienced another stab of guilt. It was all his fault. The way this whole case was going was his fault. He never made mistakes. In this business he couldn't afford to.

When he'd concocted this plan, he hadn't realized he could be vulnerable, and now it was too late to change his strategy. To all intents and purposes, she was his wife for an indeterminate period. Everything had gone according to plan, *except—*

Fortunately their friends had crowded around, denying him any more moments of agonizing self-scrutiny. Brit's parents, followed by Denise and Rod, then the guests, offered them their best wishes.

Rod, oblivious to the truth, reached the buffet table in the dining room first. His sister had to remind him to wait until the bride and groom had cut the wedding cake.

While Sid, one of the P.I.s, took pictures for their wedding album, Roman guided Brit's trembling hand to slice the first piece. Caught off guard, he almost missed the mischievous smile and glint of blue eyes seconds before a large piece of white cake found its way into his mouth.

Along with the cake, Brit's low, husky laughter, totally natural, managed to work its way past the barricades he'd erected, defeating him once more.

Entering into the spirit of the moment, he put a piece of cake in her mouth, noting inconsequentially her even, white teeth.

"You have to kiss her for the picture," Rod shouted from the sidelines. Everyone beamed at them.

"Are you ready?" he whispered.

"Are you?" Brit fired back.

It was a wicked smile she bestowed before giving him the gooiest kiss of his existence. A payback for last night. The frosting went everywhere, producing clapping and laughter. Sid snapped away. Again, Roman had difficulty believing this was all part of an elaborate con.

"Just for that, you have to clean me off."

"Yes, master."

Their eyes held as she wiped the frosting off his cheeks and mouth with painstaking care.

No words were necessary as Roman reached for another napkin and began a similar process, marveling over the subtle cleft in her chin, the pure mold of her facial structure. His beautiful madonna. That's what he'd secretly named her after first seeing her in her wedding dress.

Recognizing he was in trouble, he removed a dab of frosting from the corner of her mouth, then quickly turned away, muttering an oath to himself that the intimacy he'd enjoyed would go no further than the wedding festivities.

When they left this house in a few minutes, she'd be the client he'd sworn to protect, nothing else!

Brit had to hide her disappointment when Roman announced that he was going out for a while. It was ridiculous to have any feelings one way or the other. He was a private investigator, for heaven's sake!

This was *not* their wedding night.

They'd both been playing a part for days now. That was all.

With the supposed legalities behind them, Roman could get down to the job he'd pledged to do. She could sense his impatience to be gone.

"Lyle's on duty outside, so you don't have to worry about anything."

"I'm not," she said a little too brightly. "It's after ten and I'm awfully tired. I think I'll turn in."

"You do that. I'll see you in the morning. Sleep in as late as you want. You're on your honeymoon until next Monday morning when you show up for work."

Work.

The monumental events of this day had crowded every other thought from her mind. Even Glen Baird's horrifying image had receded for those few seconds when Roman's kiss had caused an explosion of feeling deep inside her body. Without knowing how, he'd brought her to an awareness of her femininity. She felt alive in a brand new way.

Every time she closed her eyes, she relived the passion of that magical moment until she could hardly breathe.

What she was experiencing now explained as nothing else could why she hadn't accepted Scott's proposal two years ago.

Logically, she realized this had less to do with Roman, and more to do with pure physical attraction and chemistry. Nevertheless it was the necessary ingredient lacking in her relationship with Scott.

No doubt Roman had kissed other women with just as much passion in the line of duty. He'd said he'd never played the part of a husband before, and she believed him. But she imagined his various personas occasionally required the kind of thing which they'd shared today. Of course he would never give any thought to it. Why should he?

There had to be a special woman in his life. Someone important to him when he took a night off the job to relax. The thought that he could be interested in another woman had nothing to do with Brit. *She shouldn't even be curious about what he did after hours.*

But she couldn't pretend disinterest, not when she recognized him as an exceptional human being.

Brit had always assumed an obstetrician or pediatrician worked harder, longer hours around the clock than anyone else. But only four days with Roman and she was having to change her opinions about a lot of things. Particularly about herself.

To think she'd ever wanted to be a boy.

Such naïveté was embarrassing to admit. She threw back her head impatiently. How was she going to sleep? Telling Roman she was tired was a colossal lie. She needed to talk. She needed Denise.

While she punched in the numbers, she made the decision that if Rod answered, she'd tell him she wanted to thank him for helping make her wedding special. Then she'd tell him to put his sister on the phone for a minute.

While she waited, she chastised herself and ran a trembling hand through her hair. When was she going to get it through her head that *it wasn't a real wedding*?

"Hello?" Denise answered on the first ring, sounding a trifle intense for her.

"Denise?"

"Brit! You don't know how much I've wanted to call you. I've been dying for this day to end so we could talk."

"You don't know the half of it, Denise."

"I think you've got a problem, dear friend, and I'm not talking about the psycho who's after you."

Brit couldn't speak for a minute. "You notice too much."

"Roman Lufka is kind of hard not to notice. When a man like that comes into your life, he redefines everything you thought you knew about the relationship between a man and a woman. All I can say is, be careful. His charms have even affected *me*."

There was no point in trying to lie to Denise. "He's just doing his job. All I can do is pray he never senses what I'm feeling." Her voice shook.

"That's going to be pretty hard to hide."

"I know," she moaned. "How could something like this happen? Especially now?"

"I don't know. Some men don't ask permission. They just are."

Brit reeled from the profundity of her friend's remark.

"Denise? On the way home from Mom and Dad's, Roman told me that if things look bad, he wants you and Rod to go stay with your grandparents in California while your parents are away."

"What a remarkable man, but let's hope it doesn't come to that. Oh, Brit—whoever dreamed our trip would turn into this nightmare."

"Without Roman, I don't honestly know what I would have done."

"Well I'll say this much. He's in a class all by himself. If he can't nail Glen and put him away forever, no one can. From my point of view, he's the best of the best. You couldn't ask for more than that."

"I know. Believe me. I know. I'll talk to you tomorrow."

"*Ciao*," they both said at the same time.

One more phone call to her folks, then Brit went to bed. But she spent a restless night because of the haunting male who slept a wall away.

The next morning, not long after Roman had left for work, she started acquainting herself with his house and decided to dust and vacuum to justify her existence. Up until now they'd both been preoccupied with wedding plans.

While she kept busy, her mind kept going over her conversation with Denise. So deep was her turmoil, she didn't realize the phone had been ringing.

Earlier, Roman had explained that only a handful of people knew his home phone number. All other calls were routed directly to his office and dealt with by Diana.

If that was true, then it was probably Roman calling on the cellular phone about something vital. Had the police caught up with Glen? *Please, please let it be true.*

She reached for the nearest phone in the study and picked up the receiver. "Hello?"

"*Hello, Brittany.*"

The intimate way the man greeted her, using her full name with his distinctly unwestern accent, made her blood congeal.

Sick to the pit of her stomach, she quietly put the phone back on the hook, then paged Lyle on his beeper with the cellular phone. Her hands shook so hard, it dropped on the hardwood floor.

"Brit?" he answered immediately.

"Oh, Lyle— Come inside quick. I—I think Glen Baird just tried to phone me. I was so terrified, I hung up."

"Calm down, Brit. I'm going to need backup and have to stay at my post. Here's what you do. If he's the one, he'll probably call back. I want you to keep him on the phone. It's being recorded. Get him to talk as long as you can. He may give away a few vital clues. Someone from the office will be with you shortly."

Her mouth had gone so dry, she couldn't form words.

"Brit? Can you hear me?"

"Y-yes."

"You're going to be all right. This may be the break we've been waiting for. No matter what, just keep him talking."

"All right."

She clicked off and stared at the other phone.

How could Glen have gotten Roman's private phone number? *How could he do something like that?*

She started to shiver and couldn't stop. When the regular phone rang again, she knew she was going to be ill. But she had to get it. Lyle said it might be their only lead.

Holding her breath, she gingerly lifted the receiver from the hook.

"Hello?"

"Brittany? Where did you go?"

Through wooden lips she said, "The phone dropped, and we g-got disconnected."

"Can you guess who this is?"

He was a fiend!

"I already know."

"You're too intelligent for your own good." His laughter chilled her. "I thought maybe you were scared of me, and that's why you hung up on me. Your husband knows too much, and has probably told you tales about me out of school."

She moaned. "No! I— T-that's not true. Of course I'm n-not scared of you."

"Okay. I'll forgive you, but I have to be honest. I thought you were lying about your wedding. How come I haven't heard about your plans?"

One minute had passed. If she could detain him a little longer...

"I-it's been a private affair."

"Well the cat's out of the bag now. I suppose you know you're both in serious trouble."

Her hand held the receiver in a death grip. "I was h-hoping you'd be happy for us."

"I would have been happier if you hadn't sprung it on me as a surprise. What are your favorite flowers, Brittany?"

Her body started to grow cold.

"I don't have a favorite."

"Well, you're getting some anyway. Yellow roses for besotted love? No. Red roses I think, for true love. It must be true love to have done what you've done. Besides, it's the least I can do without being there, even if they're belated."

Roses. Paralyzed with fear, Brit couldn't utter a sound.

"Is there something wrong, Brittany?"

She stifled her gasp. "What do you mean?"

"You sound upset. I'm sorry if my call has disturbed you."

"No. I-it hasn't."

"You're lying, Brittany, but I'll take that up with your husband. Say hello to him for me. Tell him I'll coming."

A new fear for Roman clutched her heart.

"Goodbye for now, Brittany."

"No!" she cried in panic. "Don't go!" But a definite click resounded in her ear.

As she put the receiver back on the hook, she heard the sound of the front door opening.

"Lyle?" she shouted hysterically.

"No. It's Roman."

"*Roman!*"

In the next breath, she was running down the hall straight into his arms.

With her head burrowed into his shoulder, her body clinging to him like a second skin, Roman had little choice except to comfort her. He nodded to Deke to go on in the study and take care of business.

Baird might be cunning. Still, Roman couldn't imagine how in the hell that maniac had traced Brit to the house, let alone come up with Roman's private phone number when only his family and the people who worked for him had access to it. Roman had covered every base. *Or so he'd thought.*

Little wonder that Brit, who up until now had been handling things with a maturity and rationality Roman could only praise, had fallen apart.

"H-he said you were in s-serious trouble, Roman." She tried to prevent the sobs racking her body. "I should never have called your company. Now he's after you. I—I couldn't bear it if anything happened to you because of me."

Over and above everything else, her fears for his safety touched him deeply. Without conscious thought he held her tighter, molding the back of her head with his hand as he attempted to reassure her.

Mistake number one hundred...

Now there'd be more things about her he wouldn't be able to erase from his mind, like the exquisite feel of her womanly body driving against his, the flowery fragrance of her silken hair and skin. He was so intent on assuaging her fear, he almost didn't realize Deke had come down the hall and was ready to exit the front door.

"It wasn't Baird, so you can relax," he murmured in an aside to Roman, a curious smile curving his mouth before he slipped out.

Relieved and satisfied that Baird hadn't traced them to his lair, Roman now felt free to indulge his curiosity.

"Brit?" He slowly eased her away from him, his hands on her slender shoulders. "Deke said it wasn't Baird."

"*What*?" came the cry of joy while those deep blue orbs, shimmering with moisture, regarded him in shock.

"Let's go in the study and find out who has upset you so much."

When Brit suddenly realized that her hands were still on his chest, a becoming red color suffused her cheeks. With a jerky motion, she stepped completely away from him. That gesture as much as anything, underlined the fact that she'd been making as earnest an effort as he had to keep their relationship on a professional basis.

Without another word she headed for the study, then stood by as he turned on the recorder.

Roman's eyes closed tightly as Yuri's voice filled the room.

Yuri!

Roman had forgotten to call him and explain. *The one thing he'd left undone too long.* But getting Brit out of immediate danger had been Roman's first priority. There hadn't been time yet, not with all the wedding arrangements to make...

He let the tape play until he heard a terrified Brit beg him not to hang up. Lyle had told her to keep him on the line any way she could.

Roman stopped the tape, then met her imploring gaze. "That was my brother."

"Yuri?" she whispered in shock. "But his voice—"

"He sounded like Baird?"

She shook her head uncertainly. "I don't know. Denise

and I ignored him whenever possible. It was only when he muttered something ugly that I noticed it at all. It was more the things your brother said. The way he said them. He called me Brittany. No one calls me that.''

"It's perfectly understandable. Even knowing it was my brother, I felt a chill when he asked you what kind of flowers you liked. The coincidence of his calling and saying the things he did about the roses, let alone the way he was teasing you like that, would have convinced anyone who didn't know Yuri that Baird was on the other end of the line.''

She buried her face in her hands, obviously trying to recapture her composure. Finally, ''I thought no one in your family knew about this assignment.''

"I thought so, too.''

The cat's out of the bag. That meant everyone in the family knew. Angela's family knew. *He'd have to call the operative over him in the CIA and fill him in.*

"Somebody at the office must have let it slip. It was probably Eric.''

Eric, bilingual in German, was without a doubt one of the best P.I.s in the business. But he had a big mouth and was a worse tease than Yuri ever thought of being. That lily was a case in point.

Eric and Roman's brother had hit it off on Yuri's first visit to Salt Lake. Since they met, Eric had been to New York twice to stay with Yuri and Jeannie.

"I have an idea my brother called the office yesterday and happened to talk to Eric who was covering for Diana so she could come to the wedding. Eric would never discuss a case with anyone, not even Yuri. But I don't put it past him to have told my brother that I was secretly married.'' Roman could imagine the conversation.

"I swear to the Almighty it's true, Yurinska. Your ba-booshka's little grandson, Romanov Lufkilovich, went and got himself an Amerikanish wife. Not a drop of Italian or Russian blood in her Ingleska veins. She'll produce some

*fine little Russkies. One day soon you'll have to come out
here and we'll all celebrate. Bring along a couple of bottles
of our favorite Siberian vodka. Ja vohl?''*

Unfortunately, in all the funning and slaughtering of
three languages, Eric had no way of knowing how his little
joke had backfired on Brit, let alone how it had sent
Roman's heart into cardiac arrest when Lyle had called to
tell Roman that Baird might have phoned Brit at the house.

The hell of it was, because Brit had thought Yuri was
Baird, she'd gone along with him to keep the conversation
alive, never denying the reality of their marriage.

If Yuri hadn't been certain that Roman had married her
when he'd first called, by the time he'd hung up the phone
Brit's comments would have convinced him otherwise.
Toward the end of their conversation, Yuri had actually
sounded repentant for giving Roman's pretend-wife the
third degree.

Under any other circumstances, Roman might have
found the situation funny, and at some point could have
even laughed about it with the guys.

But there was nothing remotely funny about this case,
about Brit, or his own tortured thoughts where she was
concerned. When he'd first come up with the idea of a fake
ceremony, he'd been confident it was the right thing to do
to get the job done. *But that was before you met Brit.*

Roman had met dozens of appealing female clients and
agents throughout his career in law enforcement and the
CIA, but he'd never felt a physical and emotional attraction
this powerful before. Granted Brit was a beautiful woman,
but so were a lot of others. He couldn't account for the fact
that her mere presence would create this kind of havoc with
his senses.

Though there'd been several women in his life, Roman
had always separated them from business. Certainly he considered the relationship between a P.I. and client sacrosanct,
and had never once stepped out of bounds.

Hell. He didn't know how he was going to do it, but

while he was waiting to catch Glen Baird, it was vital he regain his objectivity where Brit Langford was concerned.

She stared at him with a horrified expression. "Your brother probably thinks our marriage is for real."

His body tautened in response.

She's having as much trouble as I am hiding her true feelings.

"It *is* for real, as far as this assignment is concerned." His voice grated. "Anything less could jeopardize this whole operation. Forget about Yuri. I'm headed for the office and will straighten things out with Eric and my brother. Are you going to be all right?"

"Yes. Of course."

She was a valiant liar. Evidently she regretted breaking down in his arms moments ago. But not even she could be filled with as much regret as he for deciding to play the role of her husband. He'd put himself in a hole so deep, he had no idea how he was going to climb out!

Four days ago he'd been positive it was the only thing to do.

Taking a steadying breath he said, "I stopped by the post office. There was nothing in the delivery from Baird." He started for the door, then stopped. "Enjoy your fan mail," he added more curtly than he'd intended, but the knowledge that both their emotions were involved here made everything that much more complicated.

Fan mail? Brit mused.

Wounded by the abruptness of his tone and swift departure, she didn't realize he'd disappeared out the front door before she could thank him for coming back to the house to allay her fears.

With hindsight she realized that she'd made a fatal mistake when she'd rushed into his arms a little while ago. Anyone witnessing that scene could be forgiven for thinking she was his wife needing her husband's comfort and protection.

When Brit thought about it, she cringed over such impulsive behavior. No wonder he couldn't get out of the house fast enough. He was a professional through and through, trying to do his job. She, on the other hand, was the besotted idiot who'd embarrassed him in front of one of his colleagues.

What else could he do but run in the opposite direction.

Shamed by her own unconscionable actions, she determined that she would never show her vulnerable side to him again. *Never*!

Feeling at a loss because he'd gone, she took the small stack of letters sitting on the hall table and wandered into the study to read them.

Knowing that Glen Baird hadn't been the man on the phone earlier filled her with intense relief. But when she settled down to read the correspondence from several acquaintances who'd been on her tour, the pit in her stomach enlarged.

It seemed that when Glen couldn't get satisfaction from Alan and Maureen—her closest friends on the tour—he'd started harassing everyone else from their group who'd written down an address. Apparently everyone who'd heard from Glen was anxious to warn Brit that he was trying to make contact. He had to be furious that the tour group had closed ranks on him.

When she thought about it, in the eyes of the law Glen Baird had done nothing more than phone various people to get her number. Boys in high school had done the same thing.

But none of them had remotely resembled the thirty-five-year-old misfit who reminded her of a railroad transient. Knowing he'd been calling people on the tour to get her phone number made her sick.

More than ever she was thankful for Roman, for his fast thinking which had placed her out of harm's way. No matter the outcome, she would never be able to repay him for what he'd already done, let alone for what he was prepared to do to protect her.

Until Glen Baird was caught, the only thing for her to do was turn off her feelings and stay out of Roman's way as much as she could.

If you think you can do either one of those things, Brit, then you've completely lost your sanity.

CHAPTER SIX

"GOOD afternoon," Diana greeted Roman as he let himself in the back door of his office. "How's hubby today?" she teased.

"Hubby would like to get his hands on Eric for letting my bogus marriage leak to Yuri."

"That sounds like something Eric would do. But I'm afraid you'll have to wait. He's in the surveillance van at your wife's condo. Hey—you sound too grumpy for a man who just got married."

"Sorry, Diana. I think I'm tired."

"*Really.*"

Though he'd done nothing wrong, her mischievous smile made him feel guilty.

Because your thoughts aren't innocent where Brit is concerned.

"She's lovely, Roman. Cal said he wouldn't blame you if—"

"I can just imagine what your husband said," Roman interrupted her before she could finish.

He didn't mind her teasing. She was terrific and had been working for him almost from the beginning, giving him invaluable service when the time came to expand his business. Now she was the pivotal figure around which a dozen P.I.s functioned. Without her, the place would probably fall apart. But any mention of Brit and he snapped.

"What's new?"

"Your reputation has grown to the point that you don't want to know."

"You mean we have enough business to stay afloat another couple of months?"

"Very funny, Roman. Actually, I'm putting in for a raise. I thought this would be a good time since you're going to be in such a benevolent mood when you read all the faxes sitting on your desk."

"From whom?"

"Oh, various and sundry law enforcement officers, police chiefs, detectives, governors, the U.S. Attorney General, all congratulating you on your work which led to the capture of the Moffat brothers. Do I pay homage to you now, or after you've read them?"

Roman chuckled. "I should be getting down on my knees to you for keeping things running so well around the office. I couldn't do without you."

"Sure you could, but a compliment like that is always nice to hear."

"I meant it. So—anything important I need to know about before I look over the caseload that has come in this week?"

"Nothing I can't handle."

"My brother hasn't called, has he?"

"No. But Chief Wilson phoned. I left his number on your desk."

Roman liked the chief a lot. He hadn't been able to put their last conversation out of his mind.

"Thanks for speaking to the academy this morning, Roman. We've never had someone of your caliber and experience who can fire them up the way you do. I'm proud to be in uniform today. Proud to have had the privilege of knowing you and working with you on the Moffat brothers case."

"That's goes for me, too, Chief. They don't come any finer than you. Whenever you and your wife want to get away, you have a standing invitation to stay at my house. The golf course is only a half mile down the road at the foot of Mount Olympus. You'll swear you died and went to heaven."

"Better that way than in the line of duty, eh?"

Roman's features sobered. "Don't let anything happen to you. Six more months and you're home free, Chief."

"I was just about to say the same thing to you," he murmured in a curiously gruff voice. "The trouble is, you're only thirty-eight and deserve a long, happy, healthy life with a family and children. How come that hasn't happened yet?"

At the time, Roman had given him his stock answer that he was too busy to be a family man. Since working for the CIA, he never gave his personal life a serious thought. *Until now.*

Lord, what was happening to him?

"Well— if it isn't the old married man!"

Roman jerked around in time to see Cal come in the reception room and give his wife a resounding kiss. Finally he lifted his head, his eyes twinkling as he gazed at Roman. "Don't tell me the honeymoon is over so soon?" he said with blatant irony.

"I'm afraid it never happened."

"That's why you're so grumpy," Diana teased.

Cal chuckled, still holding on to his wife. "It's been all over the news about the capture of the Moffat brothers. I knew you were the one responsible. I decided to drop by and take you out for a late lunch so I could hear the details."

Roman had an idea that Cal's real motive was to hear more about Brit Langford. A taboo subject as far as Roman was concerned, *if he wanted to keep his sanity.*

"There's nothing I'd like more than to kick back with you two, but I've got some things to check out on the Baird case. However, you have my permission to take Diana for a meal. The three of us will get together later in the week for dinner."

"Don't you mean the four of us?" His friend spoke up boldly.

"No," Roman bit out abruptly without realizing it until it was too late. "Sorry about that. But don't even think it.

She's a client, nothing more. Besides, we're supposed to be on our honeymoon. I'm supposed to be keeping her all to myself."

Cal's brows lifted in silent query. "If you say so."

"I say so."

He clasped Roman's shoulder in a firm grip, conveying the kind of warmth reserved for a brother. The feeling was mutual. "Let's try to see each other before the week is out."

It came to him that he had good friends here, that Salt Lake had truly become his home. He couldn't pinpoint the exact moment when it had happened. Maybe it took Cal dropping in unannounced to realize it. *It felt good.*

The idea of having to uproot himself once more and move to South America when new orders came through from his superior was absolute anathema to him. He didn't know if he could do it.

After he saw Diana and Cal out the door, he went back to his office and started through the paperwork which took up the rest of his day. To his chagrin, he couldn't seem to concentrate. Knowing Brit was at the house alone, he wanted to go home, keep her company, have dinner with her, spend the evening with her. *Spend the night.*

You know what's wrong. You enjoy her too damn much. That's why you're going to stay at the office till late and order yourself a pizza.

After shoving himself away from his desk, he went to the kitchen and poured himself some coffee, then checked out the fax machine while he waited for Deke to report in on any news from the mobile unit. He was just on his way back to his office when he heard someone coming in through the front door.

"Roman?"

Deke had the instincts of a bloodhound, but he only sounded that excited when he'd found something really important.

The adrenaline started pumping.

"In here."

"Your hunch paid off. Eric found the maroon van with Wisconsin license plates at the hostel on West Capitol. But that's not the best news!" He burst into the room carrying a duffel bag. "Oh, ho, baby! Do you know how to call 'em!"

Always, Roman experienced the bitter with the sweet. Bitter because men like Glen Baird would continue to exist. Sweet because it felt so good to know his instincts hadn't let him down, especially not on this case which had become the most important one he'd ever taken. But right now he needed to avoid dwelling on the ramifications of that particular bit of self-discovery.

"Oh, man, Roman. It's all here. If we'd waited one more day, we'd have missed him. I'd like to patent your radar and retire."

Roman smiled grimly. "We owe Diana. She screened the initial call and sensed it was a hot one. Put the video in first. Then I'll hear the audio."

Deke hunkered in front of the TV and VCR. Over his shoulder he said, "When we took down the cameras, we found a dead cat lying in the atrium, its neck rung. The audio picked up everything."

That was Baird.

Roman felt as if he'd just been slugged in the midsection. Brit loved that cat. He wouldn't tell her about it. Instead he would buy her a new one. If he couldn't find an exact match, maybe he would look in the paper for a kitten for sale. Hopefully he could pass it off as one of Tiger's offspring.

"Baird left the west bedroom window open. His footprints were all over the place. The corner camera caught *this* as he was casing the side of the condo."

The full frontal view of the bearded man looking up at the bedroom window matched the pictures Brit had given him for identification purposes.

Roman made a sound under his breath. "The man has a total disregard for anything or anyone who gets in his way."

Deke shook his head. "It was afternoon. The management could have walked in on him at any moment."

"A deviant of his magnitude has tunnel vision, and only runs with one agenda," Roman muttered, watching some of the indoor scenes from the wireless camera hooked to the bedroom smoke alarm.

His body went rigid as he imagined Baird surprising Brit while she slept. If she hadn't come to him when she did…

"Whose tailing him?"

"Jon and Eric. They ought to be calling in pretty soon."

"Okay. Let's hear the audio."

Deke was right. The tape caught the cat's pitiful death cry, the sounds of someone in underbrush, then scraping noises and his grunt when he forced the window open. Next came Baird's voice. "You knew I was coming. You're smarter than the others—"

Roman's gaze flew to Deke's, the pupils of his eyes dilating. He rewound the tape, then played it back.

"…was coming. You're smarter than the others. You're hiding from me—"

Again Roman pressed the stop button. "There *were* others. I knew it," he said fiercely.

"Oh, man."

"Baird could very well have a pattern of stalking young women he meets on tours, then working to hoard his money until the next trip," Roman theorized. "Heaven only knows what he does when he makes contact with them."

"I'll see what I can find out," Deke murmured.

"Start in Tennessee."

"Right."

Roman listened to the rest of the tape.

"You're going to be sorry for what you did to me. So's Denise."

At the mention of Denise's name, Roman straightened to his full height.

"Deke? I'll be on the phone with Chief Bayless. We've already got Baird on a half dozen counts of breaking and entering, animal death, mail harassment, stalking. I want that pervert picked up tonight at the youth hostel and booked, his van searched. By the time I'm through with him, he'll be put away where he can't bother anybody again."

"I'm going to help you." His avowal coincided with the ringing of Deke's cellular phone.

Roman hovered in the doorway. The sudden quiet on Deke's end, his uncharacteristic pallor, was like a fist planted squarely in his gut.

"What's wrong?"

Deke put his hand over the mouthpiece. "Jon trailed Baird to a gas station, then lost him. He's hoping Eric is still on him, but he hasn't heard from Eric yet."

The image of Denise alone in her parents' house prompted Roman to action. "Tell Jon to drive to Denise Martin's house and wait for my call in his car. Then I want you to get her on the line. Baird may already know where she lives and could be headed there right now.

"Tell her not to ask any questions. Just find her brother, Rod, and drive over to my house immediately. Lyle will be watching for her to let them in. I'll call my wif—"

Too late Roman realized his slip. Deke had the good manners not to remind him he wasn't really married. "I'll call Brit and warn her they're coming."

"Right."

He punched in the numbers of his own home and waited for her to answer.

"Hello?"

Hearing her voice appealed to him far too much.

"Brit? It's Roman."

He felt her sigh of relief straight through the phone wires to his insides. "I was hoping you'd call. Is there any n—"

"Yes," he interrupted, knowing it came out too tersely, but he couldn't help it. By some strange twist of fate he'd become emotionally involved and couldn't seem to get a handle on it. "Baird came right on cue, Brit."

The silence on her end didn't surprise him. When she'd been praying it wouldn't go this far, to hear that Baird was in Salt Lake had to be shattering news. He rubbed the back of his neck. The worst of it was, he didn't know the outcome yet. But Eric was the best.

"We have pictures. We have sound. We have enough information to do damage. Brit—listen carefully. Now that Baird has shown up, I don't want Denise on her own, so you're going to have company in the next little while. She and her brother will be over shortly. Lyle will let them in."

After a tension-filled silence, "Does Rod know what's going on?"

"I'm not sure. I've decided to leave that up to Denise's discretion."

On a moan she cried, "That fiend couldn't find me, so he's gone after her, hasn't he!"

He sucked in his breath. There were some things Brit didn't need to know. This was one of them.

"My men are tailing him, but at this point I'm not prepared to take any risks. Denise will use your bedroom. You can put all your things in mine so Rod won't suspect anything. I don't think he'll mind sleeping on the Hide-A-Bed in my study. You and I will work out our own sleeping arrangements later."

More silence filled the phone wires while she worked that one out. He'd worry about it when he had the time.

"Thank you for being so concerned about them." Her voice trembled. "You're a good man, Roman Lufka."

"Don't thank me. It's my job."

"No. It's not your job. Let's be honest here. Providing refuge for Denise and Rod goes far beyond what I'm able to pay you for investigating this case. All I can say is, thank you from the bottom of my heart for doing this for them."

Her warmth reached out to envelop him. "It's my pleasure, Brit."

"I'll get things ready. When will you be home?"

"Depending on how the case proceeds, I may not be coming home tonight." *That was the only solution he could think of that made any sense.*

"Roman?"

"Yes?"

"Who takes care of you?"

He couldn't handle much more of this. She was a client. He was in mortal danger of forgetting that fact.

"I do. Good night, Brit."

Lufkilovich, you fool.

"Hi."

"Hi."

"We shouldn't keep meeting in the kitchen like this."

Brit smiled, staring at her friend out of bleary eyes. They'd been up till four talking, then had called it a night. But obviously neither one of them had been able to relax.

"Couldn't sleep, either?"

"No. Fortunately Rod doesn't suffer from the same problem."

"That's because he has no idea what is going on. I think you were wise not to tell him the truth."

"Thank goodness he likes you so much. I didn't have to ask twice if he wanted to come over for a get-together."

"That's because he's crazy about Roman," Brit whispered, but Denise heard her. "The thing is, Roman called again and said that if Glen isn't caught right away, he wants you to take Rod out of school and go visit your grandparents in California."

Denise shivered. "I'm all for that. They'll be thrilled if I call and tell them we're coming. Of course my boss at the hospital lab won't be too pleased, not when I've already had five weeks' vacation, but it can't be helped."

Brit nodded. "If it comes to that, I know Roman and I will breathe a lot easier."

"Someday I'll think of a way to repay Roman. He's like some modern day knight in shining armor."

"He's exactly like that, Denise. I'm just praying that this hero worship phase will pass. I'm already starting to panic."

"Why?" she fired back pointedly.

Brit averted her eyes. "Because he's a P.I. doing his job. Moreover I'm positive there's a woman in his life. She would have to be someone exceptional I think."

"*You're* exceptional."

"Thanks, Denise. But you know what I mean. When I asked him if he had a wife, he said no, but maybe that means he's divorced and hasn't recovered, or she died, or something."

"Maybe he's a bachelor."

"Somehow he doesn't strike me as that kind of man. He's too—" She broke off talking before she gave herself away completely.

"He's too male," Denise finished for her. "I agree."

"The thing is, if for some reason he's suffering from a broken heart, then he's probably having as much problem as *you* letting go of the past."

"Wow. Sometimes you don't fight fair."

"That's because I'm a realist, Denise. I've seen what your fiancé's death has done to you. Roman's past is a complete mystery to me. But the point is, if there was a woman, she would most likely be unforgettable or he would be married again with a family."

Denise didn't have a ready comeback. Brit knew she wouldn't have one, but the knowledge shouldn't have hurt so much. *It shouldn't hurt at all!*

"Contrary to the Brothers Grimm, dear friend, when Roman catches Glen Baird, Cinderella will not live happily ever after at the castle."

"You haven't been married long enough to make a statement like that," Denise fired back.

"*We're not married!*"

"Until Glen is caught, you *are* Roman's wife."

"You know what I mean, Denise."

"No. I don't. Tell me."

"You're choosing to be difficult."

"Because you're choosing to close your eyes to what is happening."

Brit averted her face. "I don't know what you mean."

"Oh, yes, you do. You've fallen for him. There's nothing wrong with that. You've finally met someone worthy of you. I think it's terrific."

She shook her head. "I'm only a client to him. He made that abundantly clear earlier today. Trust me, Denise. The attraction is *not* mutual."

"I don't believe you. I saw that kiss he gave you at the wedding. The sparks were flying all over the place."

"We had to make it look real." Brit's voice reverberated in the kitchen. "Besides, you're forgetting something very important."

"What?"

They stared at each other.

"Justin was a hard act to follow. In fact you haven't found anyone else you're remotely interested in since your fiancé died, agreed?"

Denise's eyes fell away. "Since it's honesty time, I'll admit that."

"Then I have to assume the same could be said of any woman Roman loved. In fact I'm beginning to think that's why he moved here from the East Coast. Do you realize he left his whole family behind? His brother, Yuri, runs the company without him, yet they're all very close.

"Denise—you should see his credentials! He had a fantastic career going in New York, yet he gave it all up and moved clear out here. No doubt he's still running away from memories." She bit her lip. "The point is, I want a man who has no past."

"Everyone has a past, Brit."

"True. But not everyone has experienced love like you

had with Justin. That's what we're talking about here. We both agree Roman Lufka is no ordinary man, either. Can you imagine what kind of woman it was who held him? Who might still hold him?

"If they shared the same kind of love as you and Justin—" Her voice caught. "Then I can't imagine anything worse than hoping and waiting and praying that someday Rom—" Brit had to pause to catch her breath. "Oh…let's just leave the subject alone."

She started banging things in an attempt to get breakfast ready. "Why don't you wake up Rod while I fix him some pancakes and sausage?"

"Make enough for me, will you?"

At the sound of Roman's voice, Brit spun around guiltily. *Had he heard them talking?*

Heat crept into her face. She flashed Denise a signal of distress. "I—I didn't realize you were home."

"I just walked in the house."

Which could or could not have been the truth. He would never tell. She couldn't bear to think he might have caught the last of her conversation with Denise.

Heavens, she didn't know how it was possible, but he was even better looking when he needed a shave. Suddenly it came to her that she was staring at him. She looked away abruptly.

"Good morning, Denise. I'm glad to see you and Rod safely installed here."

"I am, too," she responded warmly. "I'll never be able to thank you enough, Roman."

"Nonsense. This is my job."

Like Brit, Denise would never be able to pay Roman back for all his help. She, too, was full of questions, but by tacit agreement the three of them knew not to discuss the case when Rod was anywhere around.

"I'll look in on him," Roman offered, as if reading their minds. "You two finish talking. It might be a while before you see each other again, but we'll sit tight until I hear from Eric later in the day."

As soon as he disappeared out the door Denise whispered, "I hope we *do* have to go to California."

"What do you mean by that?"

"What do you think I mean? The longer you have to stay underfoot here—"

"Denise? Are you forgetting that I have to pay this man for all the luxurious round-the-clock bodyguard stuff? Already I'm in hock financially for a couple of years."

"It's obviously not worrying him. Besides, you didn't see what I saw."

"You're being cryptic again."

"You're being obtuse. I saw something in his eyes when he was looking at you just now. It disappeared when he looked at me. Don't pretend you didn't notice."

"I'm not pretending anything."

"Then you must be in shock. Not that I blame you. I can hear Maureen now. 'Hey, girls—who's that ripper bloke over there? The tall, dark one with those nice, firm muscles and all that gorgeous black hair I'm itching to run my fingers through. What is it you Yanks say? Oh yeah, that's right—he's drop-dead gorgeous. Oh, dear, I do hope Alan didn't overhear me.'"

Brit broke into laughter. She couldn't help it. If she closed her eyes, she could imagine Maureen in the room with them. They both adored the Australian woman who had been on their European tour and had become a close friend. Denise was a master of imitation and could mimic Maureen's Aussie accent to perfection. Brit could well imagine their older friend's reaction to Roman. Denise was right about that!

"You've made your point, Denise," she said, attempting to calm down while trying unsuccessfully to pour nice, even circles of batter into the frying pan.

"Oh, I hope so," she continued with her takeoff. "You know, there simply aren't that many gorgeous guys out there. The second I spotted Alan, I was knocked for nine pins and simply over the moon—''

"Oh, stop!" Brit cried out. She supposed hysteria had something to do with her mood. By now Denise had joined her.

"Can anyone come to the party or do we need a special invitation? I think Rod and I feel left out."

"Oh, they always act like that," Rod interjected. "Morning, everybody."

An affectionate and demonstrative Denise hugged her brother who probably liked it, but pretended not to care.

Roman was right behind him. To Brit's shock, he pulled Brit into his arms. Looking down at her out of enigmatic eyes more green than hazel, he said, "Good morning, Mrs. Lufka. Now that I've shaved, I'd like to greet my wife properly."

Brit's heart leaped in her chest as he lowered his mouth to hers and kissed her warmly. If it hadn't been for his brusque behavior yesterday, she might have construed this as a comfortable, welcoming kind of kiss that said, "Hello, how are you? I've had a long night. It's good to be home. I've missed you."

But she knew differently. Everything was for Rod's benefit. She schooled herself not to give anything more than a token response. If he noticed her lack of enthusiasm, so much the better. She'd made a promise to herself to keep everything on a professional level from here on out.

She heard Rod whisper to Denise, "Roman says they're still on their honeymoon."

"They are, and we're in the way," Denise whispered back.

Feeling that the charade had gone on long enough, Brit broke their kiss and eased out of Roman's arms, glancing away quickly from the probing eyes narrowed on her mouth. A thrill of excitement chased down her spine.

"Everybody to the table." Her voice shook. "Breakfast is on."

"I've got a phone call to make to the hospital lab. I'll do it from your bedroom if that's okay, Brit."

"Sure."

"Umm..." Rod uttered minutes later, working on his fifth pancake. Roman kept up with him. At this rate Brit would have to make more batter.

"You can say that again, Rod. There's nothing like homemade food. I think I'm going to love married life."

"Brit's the best! Hey, Brit? Make Roman your marshmallow squares and those tacos with the blue tortillas. They're better than anything!"

"Really?" Roman asked, his gaze flicking to her as she stood hovering over the stove.

She felt something was expected of her. "Do you like Mexican food, Roman?"

"I love it. When I lived back East, there weren't any good Mexican restaurants. My family's part Italian so we ate a lot of pasta instead."

"How come you didn't get married until now?" Rod's mouth was full of pancakes and questions that Brit didn't have the temerity to ask.

"I never had the time."

"Denise thinks it's because you fell in love with Brit and never got over her."

"She's right about that, too. Unfortunately Brit and I were too young to do anything about it in our teens. I had to move with my parents. Sometimes unavoidable separations cause changes in people's lives."

The lies rolled off his lips with such ease, Brit was staggered.

"Didn't you ever want kids?"

"I do now," Roman stated without missing a heartbeat as he poured more syrup over the last stack of pancakes.

Brit groaned inwardly and moved quickly to the sink for a glass of water.

Stop, Rod, before this question and answer session gets any more painful for all of us.

"You love Brit a lot, huh."

"Yes, I do." She felt Roman's eyes seeking hers, but she couldn't meet his gaze without giving too much of her emotions away. "We love each other very much, don't we, darling?"

Somehow Brit managed to squeak out a "yes."

"You're lucky," Rod piped up. "My sister's fiancé died in a car crash. She doesn't date anymore."

"That's because she hasn't met the right man to create new memories."

"Is that what happened to you and Brit?"

"It sure did, and it will happen to your sister one day. Just wait and see."

"There's this one guy, Pete, who just keeps calling her, but she always tells me to tell him she's not home."

"That's natural when you've loved someone else so much. Her fiancé must have been pretty terrific."

"Yeah. He was great."

"Well, give it time. Maybe deep down she likes this new guy, but is afraid of losing him, too, so she's not prepared to take the risk of falling in love again."

Rod cocked his head and looked at Roman. Obviously he hadn't considered such a possibility. "You think?"

"Maybe. Women are complicated creatures."

"You can say that again."

Brit was listening with her heart. *Was Roman referring to himself? Had he lost someone? Was he afraid to risk loving again?* She didn't know what to believe.

"Do you have a girlfriend, Rod?"

"No."

"I didn't have one at your age, either. I had too many other fun things to do with my brother, Yuri."

"I wish I had a brother."

"Well, you've got me today. How about coming downstairs? I've got a bunch of cameras and gadgets you might like to look at. My family's company makes them. James Bond stuff."

"*Cool!*"

"Let's go."

Before they got up from the table, Roman flashed her a private glance, causing her heart to turn over. "The breakfast was delicious, Mrs. Lufka," he murmured, brushing his mouth against her unsuspecting lips before he and Rod walked away.

When they were gone, she touched fingers to her mouth. For Rod's benefit, every affectionate hug and kiss had been a premeditated gesture on Roman's part to create the semblance of a happily married couple. His superb acting had pulled it off. Rod didn't have a clue. Obviously he thought Roman was the best.

Roman was the best...

He would make a fantastic father. Brit could feel it in her bones.

He already made a wonderful husband. *But you're not his wife, Brit, so don't even think about it.*

The fact of the matter was, she was single, and would probably end up an old maid. Furthermore, she was being stalked, and Roman had been hired to protect her. In terms of the emotional security he'd provided, that wasn't something you could measure in monetary value.

Financially, it would probably take her the rest of her life to pay him back what she owed.

There would be no fairy tale ending here. Period.

"Whoa... What's this, Roman?"

Roman had just come from the downstairs rest room. He'd excused himself minutes earlier to call Deke on the cellular.

Eric still hadn't called in, and until he did, everyone would be on full alert. If the finest investigator Roman had ever known had lost Baird's trail, then they had a statewide manhunt on their hands.

"That's a night vision pocket scope, Rod. The unit is a real powerhouse."

"What can it do?" Rod murmured, awestruck by all the equipment: stun guns, personal alarms, batons, locksmithing tools, two-way radios, body armor, survival products, self-defense products, recording devices, micro-recorders, bug detectors, sound amplifiers, surveillance equipment and telephone security systems. The list went on and on.

Roman saw in a glance everything Rod was looking at. He knew exactly how the teenager felt—like all his Christmases rolled into one.

"It's a starlight scope used by the U.S. troops during Operation Desert Storm. There's an automatic brightness control built in. You can see anything in the dark."

"This is so awesome!" he cried out excitedly. "The guys at school would go crazy!"

"That's an expensive piece of equipment. About four thousand dollars' worth."

"Whoa." He put the scope back on the table. "Hey? What are these?"

"They're like handcuffs, only they're called leg cuffs. They're made of heavy-duty nickel-plate with an 18-inch chain. The police use them for maximum restraint when they've captured a violent prisoner."

The more he thought about it, the more Roman wished he were back on active duty so he could be the man who put those restraints on Glen Baird.

The thought of that creep touching so much as one silky hair of her head...

If it looked like Baird was going to be difficult to apprehend, he'd send Brit back to New York to stay with Yuri and Jeannie until the fireworks were over.

Which reminded him of another problem. Not only had he not been able to find a moment to discuss the slip with Eric, he still hadn't been able to get hold of Yuri or Jeannie to tell them the truth about the situation with Brit. They weren't at the house or the office. No one seemed to know where they were.

Gossip always ran rife at home. Like feathers tossed to

the wind, it would be impossible to gather them up. He closed his eyes tightly, trying to imagine the explosion at the Riccardi household. No doubt the news had sent Angela's parents into shock.

They'd wanted Roman to marry their daughter since day one. Roman's family had wanted it, too. If Roman's life hadn't gone in a completely different direction, he might have ended up with her.

Unfortunately the longer his brother and sister-in-law remained in the dark, the more everyone who ever knew Roman back in New York would believe he had married a Utah girl.

No doubt Yuri, particularly, would be stunned by the news that his own brother hadn't even bothered to inform him of his intentions to marry. Worse, Jeannie would be hurt that he had gotten married without them, especially when he'd always maintained that being a bachelor suited his career and lifestyle.

Looking at it through their eyes, it was a callous, cruel, insensitive thing to do to them. An outright betrayal of their love.

So why aren't you trying to reach them on the phone again right now to set the record straight, Lufkilovich? What are you waiting for?

You can't answer that question, can you?

Maybe it's because you don't want to.

Maybe it's because you can still taste Brit's essence on your lips, and it's not enough. Maybe you don't want to pretend anymore.

And maybe you're out of your mind…

"Your phone's ringing," Rod called out, sporting a pair of single-tube night goggles around his head, jerking Roman back to reality with a grimace. While Roman's thoughts had been focused on Brit, Rod had turned out the lights to make the room pitch-dark, and Roman hadn't even noticed…

"Thanks, Rod."

He pulled the cellular phone from his pocket and said hello, aware that nothing like this had ever happened to him before. Definitely not during a life-and-death situation of these proportions.

"It's Deke. We still haven't heard from Eric. Chief Bayless has put out an APB on Baird per your instructions."

Roman gripped the phone tighter, and turned his back to Rod. "Good. As a safety precaution, I'm sending Denise and her brother to California on the next plane." He spoke in a low voice. "We'll be on our way to the airport shortly. Keep me informed."

"Will do. What are you going to do about your wife?"

"Very funny, Deke."

"She'd like to be your wife. I know that much."

Roman swallowed. "Since when do you have the inside track on my client?"

"Since I saw her pasted to you earlier. The last time my wife gave me a greeting like that, we were just home from our honeymoon."

"Brit was frightened."

"Tell me another story, boss. Over and out."

"Rod?" A fragmented Roman turned to him the second he'd clicked off with Deke. "I'm sorry, but it looks like I've got some business to take care of. I'll let you go through my stuff another time. Is that all right with you?"

"Sure."

"Thanks for being a good sport."

The likable teenager pulled off the goggles and handed them to Roman before they went up the stairs. Brit and Denise were still in the kitchen talking. Roman eyed Rod's sister.

"It looks like I've got to go to work. Denise, why don't you tell Rod about the early birthday surprise trip to your grandparents in California. I thought I heard Disneyland mentioned."

CHAPTER SEVEN

BOTH women jerked to attention. Brit went pale as streams of unspoken messages flowed between her and Denise.

"Are we going to Disneyland?" Rod cried out in excitement.

Denise had recovered enough to nod.

"When?"

"Today," Roman answered for her. "In fact, I have enough time to drive you to the airport if you'll hurry and get your gear together."

"That means I'm going to miss school! Cool!" he cried out with excitement and ran out of the kitchen to start getting ready.

Once Rod was out of earshot, Roman turned to Brit. "If you'll keep Rod occupied for a few minutes, I'll use the cellular phone to call the airlines and make reservations."

His gaze swerved to Denise. "You can use the phone here in the kitchen to inform your work and your grandparents. Just so you know, I'm keeping up the vigil on your parents' house in case Baird shows up there. It's purely a precautionary measure."

Denise's eyes filled. "You've done too much already. When they get back from their trip, they'll see that you're paid for all your work."

"Forget that. Until he's arrested, you need protection. If you're so worried about paying me back, then have a great vacation in California."

"Thank you, Roman. I don't know what any of us would have done without you. One day my parents and I will find a way to show you our gratitude."

On her way out of the kitchen to keep Rod secretly entertained, Brit saw her dear friend hug Roman in a spontaneous gesture of affection, one Brit craved to give him herself.

Brit may only have been around him for less than a week, but in her psyche she already recognized that he had become the most important person to her existence.

Whatever his past, she imagined there'd been a lot of women who would have given anything to be noticed by him, to spend personal time with him. Brit included. She certainly wasn't going to lie to herself about that.

However, that was as far as she would allow her thoughts to wander.

After all, she was Roman's client, nothing more. Even if he were as attracted to her as she was to him, he would be too professional to act on that attraction.

In any event, Brit wanted to be the woman who was unforgettable, the woman whose shoes no other female could ever fill.

She wanted to be number one—the hard act to follow—not the other way around. So whatever pain of loss Roman might be carrying inside him, it made no impact on her life.

With that decided, she hurried down the hall to the guest room to join Rod who immediately launched into a running commentary on all the spy paraphernalia downstairs. Already it seemed Roman had become Rod's new hero.

He didn't take that long to pack everything. Soon they joined Roman and Denise who were out in the garage, putting luggage in the trunk of his car.

"Roman?" Brit ventured because she hated being separated from him, never mind all the reasons why. "Do you think I can come along to say goodbye, or are you in too big a hurry to bring me back here before you go to work?"

His dark head lifted abruptly and their gazes locked. "Missing me already?"

He shut the trunk and started walking toward her, an enticing smile hovering at the corner of his mouth. "For that, I'll make the time."

Twice in the same morning, she found herself being given another swift kiss. It caught her completely off guard so that there was no moment of awkwardness or hesitation.

With each new day spent in Roman's company, Brit was having trouble remembering that they weren't really married.

Bemused by her feelings and Roman's vital presence, she climbed into the front seat of the car, unable to think, let alone talk.

To her relief, Rod chattered nonstop to his idol about all the spy equipment Roman had shown him. Denise, like Brit, didn't offer much in the way of conversation. She had an idea her friend was equally preoccupied by the unexpected turn of events. If Roman insisted that Denise and Rod leave today, that meant that Glen Baird hadn't been captured and was still on the loose somewhere close by.

For the last twenty minutes Brit had been so deep in thought, she'd completely forgotten about Glen. In fact, until Roman had turned off the motor, she hadn't realized they'd come to the airport, or that Roman had found a free space in the short-term parking near the doors to the sky-walk.

"I've booked you two on the next Delta flight leaving for L.A. I'll get your bags checked while the three of you go to the waiting area at gate four."

Brit was positive Roman had pulled some strings to get them on one of the regularly scheduled flights out of Salt Lake headed for the West Coast.

As the three of them passed through the security check and headed for their gate, Brit was aware of Lyle following them. Though it made her feel perfectly safe, it also reminded her that this wasn't some strange dream.

This was real. Lives were in danger.

Roman was a P.I. doing his best to keep her and Denise out of harm's way. But one more kiss and Brit knew she would be in real danger of an entirely different kind. She didn't dare put a name to it.

Rod chose that moment to comment on how great Roman was, how much he loved being with him. Just then Denise flashed Brit a meaningful look. To Brit's embarrassment, a blush crept over her face, giving away her guilty secret. She started walking faster.

"What's the hurry?" a deep, familiar male voice spoke behind her. In the next instant, she felt Roman's arm slide around her shoulders, causing her body to quicken in acknowledgment.

She absolutely refused to look at him, and tried to quell the frantic beating of her heart, but her breath still came out haltingly. "I—I just wanted to be sure they don't miss their flight."

"There's no danger of that," he whispered near her ear, sending little shivers of delight through her nervous system. "The plane barely arrived from New York."

It was true. They'd reached the waiting area in plenty of time. The place was packed to the brim with people getting ready to board, as well as those persons thronging to greet debarking passengers. There were no vacant chairs anywhere, forcing them to stand.

Rod glommed on to Roman. "I wish you were coming with us."

"I do, too, Rod. I've never been to Disneyland."

"You're kidding!" everyone else said at the same time.

Roman chuckled. "No. It's something I've always wanted to see, but never got around to doing."

"When you and Brit have kids, you can take them."

"I was thinking the same thing, Rod," Roman murmured, tightening his arm around Brit as he spoke.

The idea of having Roman's children sent another charge of electricity through her trembling body.

"Are you all right?"

"Y-yes," she lied. "Of course."

"We're going to catch Baird," he whispered.

To her shame, she hadn't been thinking about Glen.

Roman was the man who occupied her thoughts until

there was no room for anything else. What would it be like
to be loved by him, create a family with him?

"I know that," came her lame response at long last.

"It's just a matter of ti—"

"*Romanov Lufkilovich*? Over here!" she heard a male
voice call out above the din of voices, interrupting the last
of Roman's response.

She felt his head swerve in the direction of the line of
people deplaning. Almost immediately she spied an attractive man and woman moving toward them as fast as the
crowd would allow.

The man was shorter than Roman, a little heavier, but he
had his brother's dark, good looks. Brit would have recognized him anywhere.

She heard Roman mutter something undecipherable.
"It's Yuri and Jeannie— *What in the hell are they doing*
here? No wonder I couldn't reach them on the phone!"

Roman's hand tightened on her shoulder, probably without his realizing it. "Continue to play the role of my wife
until I tell you otherwise," he demanded before ushering
her forward.

"Eric was supposed to keep our arrival a surprise!" Yuri
spoke to Roman with a grin on his good-looking face. "I
should have known he wouldn't be able to keep his big
mouth shut, but I'm not sorry you're here to greet us. It's
good to see you, you sly old fox."

Within seconds the two brothers were embracing with
such heartfelt warmth, Brit felt a lump in her throat.

The vivacious auburn-haired woman at his side rushed
over to hug Brit. "You're Roman's new bride. I can't tell
you how absolutely thrilled I am."

Brit hugged her back, unable to do anything else until
Roman gave her permission.

Dear God. No wonder Roman was so upset. He hadn't
yet had a chance to tell his brother and sister-in-law the
truth about their bogus marriage. Unfortunately the lie

would have to go on a little longer, at least until Rod and Denise boarded the plane.

"All right." Yuri's voice could be heard above the others. "Now let me have a look at the woman who accomplished the impossible and snared my little brother when everyone said it couldn't be done."

Yuri let go of Roman and turned to Brit, a definite gleam of male admiration in his eyes as they swept over her.

"You're even more gorgeous than I had imagined. Welcome to the family, Brittany." Then she was engulfed by arms every bit as powerful as Roman's.

"Have you forgiven me yet for teasing you on the phone the other day? I'm afraid you've married into a rather unique family. Jeannie can tell you all about us, can't you, darling—"

He turned adoring eyes to his wife who appeared equally enamored of her husband.

Brit could understand the other woman's feelings since Roman brought out that same sort of emotion in her, Brit.

"Yuri? Jeannie?" Roman spoke up before Brit could say anything. "Allow me to introduce Denise and Rod Martin. Denise is Brit's oldest and dearest friend, and Rod is her brother. They're on their way to Disneyland. We were just seeing them off."

When all the introductions were made, Rod squinted up at Yuri. "Did you really plant a bugging device in Jeannie's car before you got married so you could spy on her?"

"*What*?" Jeannie cried out. The astonishment on her face had to be genuine.

Suddenly Yuri's head reared back and he laughed out loud, giving everyone his answer.

"You really did that?" Brit cried out in horror.

"You don't want to know the half of it," Roman murmured wryly. At this point he'd wrapped his arms around Brit's waist from behind, his chin resting in her hair, giving more credence to the lie that they were married. The feel of his hard body, the closeness, sent her into shock.

Jeannie shook her head, but Brit could tell the other woman was having trouble holding back the laughter. "You'd better get used to it, Brit. If I were you, I'd never say anything I didn't want Roman to hear, especially to an empty room. His house contains every surveillance device known to mankind."

Brit had suspected as much, and died another little death when she thought of her conversation in the kitchen with Denise earlier that morning. *What if it were on tape and Roman listened to it?*

As if he could read her mind, his grip tightened so she couldn't move.

"Roman told me that as soon as we get back from California, he'll attach one of those tracking cameras to my dog's collar so I can see where he goes."

At Rod's comment, everyone broke into laughter, including Brit.

Yuri flashed his brother a devilish glance. "I don't suppose you told them about the time unbeknownst to our mother when you put a camera on the hood of the car so Dad could find out where *she* went all day long."

"*That's terrible!*" Brit and Denise blurted at the same time.

Being held this close to Roman, Brit could feel his body shaking with suppressed laughter.

"*Passengers are now boarding for flight 1160 to Los Angeles. Please have your boarding passes ready.*"

Denise darted a searching glance at Brit. "I guess this is it."

Roman allowed Brit to leave his arms so she could hug her friend. "Call me as soon as you get there, Denise. *Please*—" she whispered shakily. "I have to talk to you."

"I promise. Take care."

"Have a wonderful time, Rod," Brit murmured.

"I will. But when we get back, can I come over and see some more of your stuff, Roman?"

"Sure you can. Anytime."

Brit accompanied them as far as she was allowed. When they disappeared through the walkway, she turned to Roman, wanting him to explain the truth about everything to his brother and sister-in-law before any more time passed.

To her shock, Roman had *vanished*!

"What happened to your brother?"

"Relax." Yuri smiled. "He went for the car. We'll meet him outside the terminal. Don't worry. The way you two were holding on to each other a minute ago, he won't be long. I can remember when Jeannie and I were newlyweds. She used to fall apart every time we were separated, too."

Was Brit's attraction for Roman that obvious?

Jeannie gave her husband a peck on the cheek, then put her arm through Brit's and they started walking ahead of him.

"Roman looks ten years younger and so much in love, I hardly recognize him," Jeannie confided. "You can't imagine how happy this makes me. I adore Roman almost as much as I do Yuri. They're the two most wonderful men in the entire world. Obviously you found that out already, otherwise you wouldn't be married to him."

Brit groaned inwardly, wishing Roman hadn't left her alone with them. But maybe he hadn't had a choice. The more she thought about it, the more she realized there must have been a new development in the case. Maybe Lyle had received word about Glen, and Roman was conferencing with the other P.I.s.

Unfortunately there seemed to be no stopping Jeannie who remained oblivious to any undercurrents and leaned closer to Brit in a manner of longtime friends.

"When you're ready to tell me, I want to hear everything. You know. How you met, when he proposed. Ever since Eric told us the news, we haven't been able to think about anything else. We want to take you out for a fabulous dinner tonight and really celebrate."

"I—I'm afraid you'll have to consult Roman on that," Brit answered nervously.

Jeannie chuckled. "I realize you're still on your honeymoon and Roman wants to hide you away for himself, but because he kept your wedding a secret, he's going to have to suffer the consequences and share you with us sooner than he'd planned. You don't mind, do you?" she asked with a trace of anxiety.

Jeannie would make anyone the perfect sister-in-law, but right now Brit was in agony. "Of course not."

"I'm glad you said that because Yuri probably wouldn't take no for an answer."

If he was anything like Roman, then Brit understood exactly what the other woman meant.

"Eric said something about Roman being on an important case, which was why you hadn't gone on a real honeymoon yet. Yuri and I thought maybe we could all use this time to get better acquainted until Roman is free to take you away for a while."

"T-that's very thoughtful of you," Brit barely managed to respond as they passed through the doors to the outside of the terminal.

"Now that he's married, my secret hope is that you'll influence him to cut down on his caseload and come back to New York more often. Our children miss him horribly. We do, too."

"He misses you very much," Brit replied honestly. "Roman and Yuri seem exceptionally close, even for brothers."

"Oh, they are. It about killed my husband when Roman pulled up stakes. On the other hand, he finally realized what Roman was up against and supported that decision, even when no one else could believe he would walk away from everything he ever knew and start all over again someplace else."

Up against?

Brit had no idea what Jeannie meant, but was afraid she wouldn't like it when she found out what it was.

Jeannie gave her another hug. "The past doesn't matter anymore. Obviously his move to Utah has proved to be inspirational because he met and married you. Promise me you won't let anything that old friends or family say about Roman leaving New York because of Angela bother you. None of it matters one iota because I can tell that my brother-in-law is madly in love with you. No one else's opinion counts."

There *was* another woman. *Angela*...

All along Brit had known it, but somehow hearing it from Jeannie made it too real and set up an ache in Brit's heart that wouldn't go away.

She wanted to know more, and would have asked Jeannie for an explanation, but Roman's tan car had pulled up in front. They all climbed inside and he drove off looking preoccupied, his features set and hard.

While he'd gone for the Ford in the carpark, he must have heard from one of the other P.I.s and the news wasn't good. Glen Baird was still on the loose and so far had managed to elude everyone. Brit could feel it. She shivered in place.

Yuri leaned forward and patted Roman's shoulder. "Hey—why so intense?"

"There've been some developments in a case I'm working on. I need to get to the office. Brit will drive you home. I don't know when I'll be able to join you."

Through the sideview mirror Brit could see Phil's Chevrolet trailing a couple of cars behind. She wasn't worried about her own safety. Being with Roman had made her feel invincible. Roman's welfare was foremost on her mind.

Though she would have preferred him to use this time to tell his brother and sister-in-law the truth of their situation—that she was a client who had hired Roman to protect her, nothing more—she could see that now wasn't the time to bring it up.

Roman continued to drive over the speed limit all the way to his office in the Foothill area. It was a miracle they weren't pulled over by the police.

En route he allowed Yuri and Jeannie to say and think what they wanted, letting the two of them dominate the conversation. Sooner than she would have believed, he pulled around the back of an end suite in the Foothill Complex and jumped out of the car, the engine still idling.

"I'll see you when I see you." His gaze flicked from his family to Brit, the expression in his eyes indecipherable before he turned sharply away and let himself in the back door with a key.

Brit ran around to the driver's side and got behind the wheel. She would have given anything to know what Roman had learned. As it stood, she would have to be patient until he made contact on the phone, or better still, came home.

"Okay—" Yuri began. "We want to hear everything. Chapter and verse. Don't leave out any of the good parts."

"Darling!" his wife chastised him, but Brit knew Jeannie was just as eager as her husband for every detail of Brit's courtship with Roman.

"If you'll wait till we get home, I'll tell you everything," Brit promised. Whether Roman liked it or not, she couldn't live such a colossal lie any longer. He loved and trusted Yuri. Surely it would be all right to reveal the true facts of the situation to his brother.

"You look as tense as Roman, Brit. Don't worry about him. He can take care of himself better than any human I know. Among other things he trained as a Green Beret."

Brit imagined as much.

But as far as she was concerned, Glen Baird was certifiably insane, which made him dangerous to everyone, even Roman.

Foothill wasn't that far from the Mount Olympus area.

With the aid of the remote, Brit was able to drive the Ford into the garage. She pushed the remote again and saw Phil's car drive past as the big door closed behind them.

Once they'd gone inside the house with their luggage and freshened up in the guest bathroom, she invited them to sit down in the living room and offered them sodas which they accepted with pleasure.

Yuri shed his suit jacket and tie and relaxed in Roman's favorite leather lounging chair. Jeannie curled up in one corner of the sofa opposite Brit who preferred to sit on a straight-back chair in front of them.

Through Yuri's veiled eyes she saw the gleam. "All right. We've been good little boys and girls. Now it's treat time."

Brit's mouth curved upward. She was already charmed by Jeannie's husband, too. There was something about the Lufkilovich men...

You're going to have to get over him, Brit.

Straightening in the chair she said, "Actually, Roman and I aren't married."

She might just as well have dropped a bomb. They looked totally shell-shocked.

Yuri sat forward, all mirth gone. His crestfallen expression reminded her of a little boy who'd asked for a train for Christmas and was given a book on trains instead.

"You mean you're living together but told everyone you were married."

A deep sigh escaped. "We're living together, but not in the sense you mean. I hired him to protect me from a man who has been stalking me."

A long silence ensued. She could hear their minds working, making adjustments.

"You're serious?" Jeannie finally cried out, whether from shock, disappointment, horror, or all three, Brit couldn't tell.

Yuri shook his head. "I don't believe you. Eric told me you two got married at your parents' house."

''We did, but it was one of the P.I.s who married us to make it look real. Because of this madman who is after me, Roman felt the best way to protect me around the clock, *and* keep my reputation intact, was to go undercover as my husband. I'm afraid Eric played a joke on you without telling Roman. I'm so sorry.''

''But you didn't deny it when I phoned you.'' Yuri sounded pained.

''I know. Because I thought the stalker had traced me to Roman's house and knew the phone number. One of the P.I.s told me to keep you talking on the phone so they could trace it. I-it's a long story.''

By now Yuri was on his feet, pacing. Then he stopped and impaled her with stormy green eyes reminiscent of Roman's. ''I still don't believe it. I know my brother. He's in love with you.''

Brit shook her head. ''No. What you saw at the airport was good acting. The boy you met, Denise's brother, has no idea that I'm being stalked.

''That's why Roman kept up the pretense as long as he did in front of Rod. You see, Denise could be in danger, too. Roman sent them to California where they'd be safe. Rod thought his sister had decided to take him on a vacation while their parents are away.

''Roman had no idea you were on that plane. I think he was as shocked as you are now.''

With a solemn expression, Jeannie got to her feet and linked her arm through her husband's. She stared at Brit in a daze. ''Yet you and Roman act like a man and wife who are crazy about each other.''

Brit averted her eyes. ''Looks can be deceptive. Don't forget—Roman is a master P.I.''

There were times when Roman had almost fooled Brit. But now that she knew about Angela, Brit had cast the blinders aside. A little dose of reality went a long way.

''Surely you must realize that if it had been a real wedding, you two would have been the first people to know about it. Roman adores both of you and would have insisted on your being part of the festivities.''

Yuri still didn't seem convinced.

Deciding to take the plunge she added, ''Though he's never discussed it with me, it's obvious that Roman still has feelings for the woman he left behind. I believe you called her Angela, didn't you, Jeannie?''

The other woman blinked, then slowly nodded. ''We've hoped and prayed for so long that he'd get over her and find someone else. When we heard about you, we couldn't contain our joy. That's why we rushed out here! You seem so perfect for him. It's hard to believe none of this is true.''

She turned to her husband. ''Why would Eric lie to us like that? We've flown all the way out here at the most inopportune moment for Roman. Right now I'm so angry I can hardly speak.''

Her husband shook his head. ''That's the trouble with jokesters. They sometimes go too far. Eric really did it this time.''

''Please—'' Brit spread her hands. ''It's not the end of the world. I'm sure Eric didn't mean any harm. Roman admitted to me he's never pretended to be someone's husband before. I'm sure his colleagues found it amusing.

''Eric had no way of knowing that the minute you heard, you'd drop everything to come out here and celebrate with Roman. And even if you did, I know how much he loves you. He talks about you all the time and doesn't need a reason to be thrilled to see his family!''

She didn't seem to be getting through to them. ''Y-you're both acting like this is a funeral. It's not!''

Just keep telling yourself that, Brit, until you believe it.

Yuri's eyes glinted with admiration and something else she couldn't decipher. ''You're a very generous, beautiful woman. If my brother has any brains at all, he'll make your marriage real.''

''You're embarrassing her,'' Jeannie whispered, but Brit

heard her. "For all we know, Brit's been taken by another man."

"No," she assured them.

"Why not?" Yuri fired back.

"I've been so busy establishing a career as an architect, I guess I haven't been looking for one. That's probably the reason I ran to Roman for help in the first place."

"But you like my brother."

Like?

The words caught in her throat. "It's more a case of being so thankful for him, I'm afraid it borders on worship."

Suddenly she saw Yuri's white smile, reminding her of another smile which had the power to turn her heart over and over again. "That's a start!"

She laughed softly. Yuri was incorrigible. The trouble he and Roman must have gotten into when they were young didn't bear thinking about.

Before Yuri got any more ideas she said, "Wonderful as Roman is, he has a past. I intend to end up with a man whose past, present and future are all tied up in me and me alone. My best friend says that's impossible, but I guess I'm one of those idealistic kinds of people who remains optimistic that he's somewhere to be found in the cosmos."

That's putting it out front. Bluntly. Now you can't go back on it.

"It's every woman's dream," Jeannie concurred. "Hang on to it."

Yuri was oddly quiet. "If you'll excuse me, Brit, I'm going to take a short nap in the guest bedroom. Do you want to join me, Jeannie?"

"Please—" Brit intervened before Jeannie could say anything else. "Both of you—do whatever you do when you visit Roman. I'm going to be in the study sketching some designs for a new client. You have much more right than I to be here. I'm sure Roman would tell you to make yourselves at home. I'll see you later."

She took their empty glasses to the kitchen and washed them out before heading for the den.

Maybe it was a good thing they'd come. Their presence brought Brit back to a semblance of reason and sanity. Another day, another night alone with Roman in this house, and she was on the verge of making a total fool of herself where he was concerned.

CHAPTER EIGHT

THE sun had long since dipped below the horizon when Roman and Sid finally heard from Eric and raced up Alta Canyon in the Wasatch Mountains east of the city.

Roman noticed a ShopWise truck pulled to the side of the road before they came upon an abandoned mine shaft maybe a block further on where the P.I. had trailed Glen Baird. Lights from a dozen police cars, a fire truck and a SWAT team van flashed around the opening.

Roman jumped out the passenger side and approached the big blond German. "Have they brought him out yet?"

"No. They're going to tear gas him. The tunnel doesn't go back very far. They'll flush him out before too long."

"I knew you wouldn't lose him."

"Ahh.... I wasn't so sure. It was luck, Roman. Pure luck. Jon saw him abandon his van at the gas station and run to the adjacent mall where he disappeared in that huge ShopWise store on 72nd.

"While Jon covered the front, I circled around the back, figuring he'd run out the rear door. Nobody appeared. Pretty soon the garage door to the docking entrance opened and a ShopWise truck emerged. From my angle, I couldn't see the driver, but he shot out of there too fast for someone who should be watching out for foot traffic.

"That tipped me off it could be Baird, so I followed the van. When it started up the canyon, I had an idea I was on the right track. Unfortunately, the battery in my cellular had worn down and that's why I couldn't contact anybody. There were batteries in the glove compartment, but during the chase I didn't have time to put them in.

"When he pulled off to the side of the road beyond the

ski lift area, I figured it was Baird. I hid my car behind some pines. As soon as he jumped out of the van and looked around, I had a positive ID.

"He started for the mine ahead. I crept up on him and saw him disappear into the shaft. That's when I fixed the phone to call for police backup and inform you."

Roman sucked in his breath before clapping him on the shoulder. "You did great work, Eric."

"Ja? Well I knew this was a special case."

There was no room for pretense. "It is," Roman's voice rasped with emotion.

That monster would never terrorize Brit or anyone else again.

"Sid can ride back with me. We'll handle things from here on out. Why don't you go on home and tell your wife she's out of danger," Eric suggested with a twinkle in his eyes.

Roman nodded, deciding to let the teasing comment pass. Earlier he'd wanted to take Eric to task for telling Yuri something that patently wasn't true. But right now he was so relieved that hairy-faced pervert was about to be arrested, he didn't have the heart to rip into Eric. Not when he'd brought Baird down.

With hindsight Roman felt somewhat responsible anyway. He should have taken the time to phone Yuri in the first place and tell him about his latest case so he wouldn't be surprised if Brit answered the phone.

"One more thing before I leave, Eric. Baird could be a serial stalker. Maybe he keeps pictures of all the women in his van."

Eric's brows lifted. "I wouldn't doubt it. I'll look into it."

"Call me at home later and give me a rundown."

"*Ja vohl,*" he called out as Roman made his way to the company car.

Sid had left the keys in the ignition. Roman started up

the motor and headed down the canyon for home. He couldn't wait to tell Brit her nightmare was over.

But he hadn't gone five miles when his euphoria changed to something else. *As soon as she learns Baird has been taken into custody, there'll be no more reason for her to stay with you. Tomorrow she'll move back to her condo and you'll move on to another case.*

Roman pressed on the accelerator. She hadn't even heard the news, let alone packed up her things and left. Yet Roman was experiencing a horrifying sense of loss. *One week.* That was all it had been, but he felt like Brit's advent into his world had altered it beyond recognition.

There were certain signs she'd given that she was more than a little attracted to him, but he couldn't possibly ask her to stay on. For a dozen different reasons—all legitimate and moral—it was out of the question.

Even if you decided to break every rule, you still have no right to ask or expect anything of her when you're involved in CIA affairs. Better to cut it off clean, the way you've done with all your other cases. No mess. No fuss. No aftermath.

Just...emptiness.

The closer he drew to his house, the larger that emptiness yawned until he was swallowed up by it.

So deep was his turmoil, when he came in from the garage, he didn't realize Yuri was waiting for him in the hallway until he heard his name called.

Roman's head jerked around. His brother's sober expression stopped him cold.

"We've got to talk, buddy."

He rubbed the back of his neck absently. "You're right. But first I need to see Brit."

"Is there any word on the man who's been stalking her?"

Nonplussed, Roman stared at Yuri. "Brit told you."

Yuri nodded grimly. "Everything. Even the fact that she's not your wife. I could wring Eric's neck."

A deep sigh escaped. "Don't blame him too much. I should've called you and told you what was happening, but because of the time restraints involved, her case took top prio—"

"*Roman*?"

Over Yuri's shoulder he saw Brit timidly enter the foyer with Jeannie at her heels. Brit looked pale. Quite a different greeting from the last time when she flew into his arms.

Is that what you were hoping for tonight? Did you really think it would happen a second time?

"Baird is in the hands of the police as we speak, Brit. It's over."

Their gazes fused. She looked like a person who'd gone into shock. "You're serious."

"I am," he answered in a thick-toned voice. "Why don't we all go in the living room and I'll tell you everything."

"That's wonderful!" Jeannie cried out and gave Brit a hug before the four of them left the hallway. It didn't surprise Roman that Jeannie was already on such a friendly footing with Brit.

A warmhearted person by nature, his sister-in-law had been under the impression for several days that Brit was his wife. She'd been prepared to love her unconditionally.

Yuri wasn't any different. The news that they weren't married had come as a blow to his brother. Roman could feel his disappointment and understood why.

When Roman moved to Salt Lake, his brother thought he was grieving for Angela who'd ended up marrying Roman's good friend, Frank Berkowitz. Like all his old friends, plus everyone else in the family, he assumed Roman's heartache had been so great, he'd decided to pull up stakes and relocate to try to get over the pain.

For them to hear through Eric that Roman had fallen in love with another woman and married her would have thrilled Yuri and Jeannie.

Roman knew how much his brother wanted him to get married and have a family—a normal life. Because of this knowledge, there'd been many agonizing moments in the past when Roman suffered guilt over the choice he'd made to work for the CIA.

At the time he'd been approached while serving in the Marines, Roman had looked upon it as a kind of culmination of the adventurous life, one he'd openly embraced since his teens. It had been an easy decision because though he'd dated his share of women, there was no special woman in his life.

Once inducted, he couldn't see marriage fitting into the scheme of things. He had no desire to expose a wife and children to the inherent dangers of being tied to a man who led a double life. It would make him too vulnerable. It made no sense. Much to Yuri's chagrin, Roman had remained single.

Nothing's changed. You're still single. So how come you feel like you're getting ready to go through a divorce you don't want?

"W-where did they catch him?" Brit wanted to know the second they were all seated around the coffee table.

"In Alta."

"*What?*"

Her astonishment intensified the blue of her eyes, making it impossible for him to look anywhere else.

"Eric followed him up there."

For the next few minutes Roman explained what had happened, patiently answering her questions until she was satisfied that it was truly over. "He'll never bother you or anyone else again."

Yuri clapped his hands on his thighs. "I think this calls for a celebration. Why don't we all go out to dinner?"

"You took the words right out of my mouth, big brother. Where would you like to eat, Brit?"

To his surprise, she'd gotten to her feet. Avoiding his eyes she said, "That's very kind of you to offer, but you've done too much for me already. I'll be in your debt forever." Her voice shook.

"Since it's not too late, I'm going to call my parents, who've been anxious, and ask them to come and get me. I'll stay with them until I move back into my condo. Next week I'll get paid and send you the first installment on the bill.

"Please—don't let me interfere with your plans. Yuri—Jeannie—" She turned to them. "It's been wonderful meeting you, getting to know you. Now that Roman's back, I realize you'd like to spend some private time with him.

"If you all want to leave now, don't worry about me. I'll let myself out later, after I've done a little cleaning up and packed my bags."

Roman felt as if he'd just been cut off from the light and tossed into an inky, bottomless void.

Brit flew out of the living room and headed for Roman's bedroom where she'd slept last night. *Alone.* She flung herself across the bed and buried her face in it to stifle the sound of her convulsion.

The case was over. She had no more reason to stay under Roman's roof.

The thought of going back to her empty condo was tearing her apart. In a week's time she'd grown so used to being with Roman, she couldn't imagine her life without him.

She'd fallen in love with him. Hopelessly. Irrevocably.

Furious with herself for giving in to her emotions, she sat up and wiped her eyes with her arms. That's when her gaze caught the glint of the diamond sparkling from her ring finger. No, not *her* diamond. The diamond Roman had whipped out to make everything look real.

She remembered the night he'd put it there. It had felt so right when he'd slid it home. Then his mouth had descended. Though she'd only known him a few hours, oh, how she'd wanted to respond. It had taken all her willpower not to deepen their kiss and forget everything else.

As foolish as it might sound to anyone else, when she'd walked into the police station and had first laid eyes on

Roman, it was as if he was the man her heart had been holding out for.

But the same experience hadn't happened to Roman. Another woman had a stranglehold on his emotions, and he'd only been carrying out the job Brit had hired him to do. To stop Glen Baird from torturing her...

Brittany Langford! How can you be feeling so sorry for yourself when he has just told you that maniac will never harass you again—when he has put his life on the line for you, never once thinking of his own safety—

Because of Roman, you're free from fear, you ungrateful wretch!

You should be crying tears of gratitude and thanksgiving!

You're a mess!

You don't deserve this great blessing!

A soft rap on the door made her jump. She got to her feet praying there were no signs of tears left on her undoubtedly ravaged face. "Yes?"

"Brit?" came the deep voice she loved. She *loved*.

"Yes, Roman?"

"Have you already called your parents?"

"I—I was just about to."

"When you talk to them, tell them I'll drive you over to their house. I have to go downtown anyway and meet Eric there. It will probably be an all-nighter. En route, there are still a few things we need to discuss. All right?"

No. It's not all right. I'm terrified again, but it's because I'm afraid you'll sense what I'm trying to hide from you.

"Brit— What's wrong?"

"N-nothing. In fact I'm wonderful," she lied, experiencing another painful lurch of her heart. "I guess I'm still in shock."

After a sustained pause he said, "You don't need to pretend with me. I know you're worried, but you don't have to be. I'm not going to make you face Baird. You've already given your information to the police. What you have to do now is to put this incident behind you."

Her eyes closed tightly. He was always concerned about her welfare, always putting her needs first.

"Thank you, Roman. I appreciate that more than you know. I'll tell my parents you're bringing me home. Give me about ten minutes and I should be ready to go."

It took her more like a half hour. By the time she'd contacted her folks who were overjoyed that the reign of terror was over, she started gathering up everything to pack.

What a joke— Her stuff was all over the house, *like she belonged there*!

Everytime she found something of hers in an unlikely spot—such as one of her hair clips in the kitchen by the toaster—it was a wrench to have to remove it, knowing this was the last time she'd be in this room fixing Roman's breakfast.

She found it even more difficult to straighten the study. Her clutter from the office lay everywhere. Roman had never said one word except to order her to make herself at home. Brit preferred his study to any other room in the house because it contained books and paintings and artifacts he loved. There were dozens of little framed pictures on the mantel of him and his family, at all different ages.

If she didn't think lightning would strike her, she would steal the one of Roman when he was about seventeen years old, obviously a high school heartthrob, already at his full height looking incredibly fierce and fit in a karate outfit, his fists in the air. A young man who wanted to live his life on the edge and had managed to fulfill his dreams.

"I didn't see Jeannie or Yuri," she said by way of conversation as they drove away from his house, her bags packed in the trunk. There was a tension between them she hadn't felt before, making it awkward for her to produce desultory conversation.

"Since they knew I probably wouldn't be home until

morning, they decided to go to dinner by themselves.'' His voice sounded unusually bleak.

"I—I'm sorry this case caused complications for you with your family. I know you'd rather be with your brother than anything.'' She stared out the passenger window, afraid to even look in his direction.

"Don't apologize for something that wasn't anyone's fault. Yuri and I see plenty of each other. This is a nice vacation for them without the children, much as they love them.''

"They're wonderful people, Roman.''

"I agree. Now, let's talk about your situation. First thing in the morning, I'll phone your landlord and tell him you're ready to move back in. Then I'll contact the movers, post office and utilities and have them call you tomorrow at your parents', or at work, to arrange times to come to the condo that meet with your schedule.''

"Thank you,'' she whispered, dying a little more with every word he spoke because it meant she was drifting farther and farther away from him.

Too soon they arrived in front of her parents' home. Before he'd even turned off the ignition, she'd pulled the ring from her finger.

More than a little short of breath she murmured, "This is valuable. Let me give it to you before I forget.''

Roman stared down at the ring lying in her extended palm. She couldn't understand the hesitation before he reached for it, clasping it in a fist before slipping it in his front trouser pocket.

The brush of his fingers against her skin electrified every cell in her throbbing body. If she could hear her heart pounding in her ears, *he* probably could, too.

Mortified by her reaction, she opened the door and climbed out, anxious to remove herself from his all-searching gaze.

He *had* to know how she felt about him. But he was

probably used to women falling in love with him and didn't let it phase him. The gentleman to the bitter end...

She reached the trunk in time to pick up her train case so he wouldn't have to carry everything she'd brought with her. He'd done more than enough.

When they climbed the steps to the front porch she wheeled around and faced him. "I can handle everything from here."

His eyes, more black than hazel in the dim porch light impaled her. "Not until you've opened the door and I see you safely inside."

Fumbling for the key, she finally found it and inserted it in the lock, then opened the door. Roman placed the bags inside the door.

Brit heard her mother's voice, urging her to bring Roman on in.

No! No more!

"He can't, Mom," Brit called without consulting Roman. "He has to go down to police headquarters!"

A tiny nerve near his temple throbbed. She noticed that it only did that when he had something vastly important on his mind. Though *she* could forget Glen Baird, Roman had a night's work ahead of him. In fact she had an idea he planned to interrogate him and was anxious to get going on the gruesome task.

Far be it from Brit to detain him.

Staring no higher than his chin she said bravely, "There aren't any words to thank you for what you've done. Send me the bill as soon as you've figured out all the expenses. If it takes me the rest of my life, I'll pay you back what I owe you. But it will never be enough." Her voice trembled. "God bless you, Roman."

Before she broke down, she hurried inside and closed the door. The last thing she saw before it clicked shut was the stonelike set of his handsome, rock-hard features, permanently etched in her memory.

* * *

The sun peeking over the mountaintops stung Roman's bleary eyes as he turned into his driveway. It had been the night from hell.

Certainly the evidence turned up by the crime lab after searching Baird's van gave the experts enough fodder in the form of pictures, maps and travel brochures to open up a half dozen unsolved stalking incidents in various states.

Sickened by the sight of Baird who was definitely a candidate for a mental institution if not life imprisonment, Roman decided to let Eric take over the interrogation.

He was the one who'd trailed Baird to the mountains. Roman and he conferred several hours while Baird was being booked, deciding on the best strategy to get information out of him. But the whole time they were talking, Roman's mind kept replaying the events after he'd come back home from Alta, those tension-packed scenes with Brit which were still torturing him until he felt an unspeakable sickness threatening.

Dear God. He felt as if he'd lost something vital to his very existence. It was unlike any other feeling he'd experienced in his thirty-eight years.

You made your initial mistake when you decided to play the role of her husband.

The problem with you, Lufkilovich, you don't know when to turn it off and on anymore. You've been acting out a part so long, you don't even know who you are or what's real—

"Good morning."

"Yuri!" Roman stopped in stride as he entered the kitchen from the hallway, intent on a stiff whiskey to numb the pain. "It's not even seven. What are you doing up?"

"Waiting for you so we could have that talk."

He went to the kitchen cabinet above the microwave and reached for the Jack Daniel's.

"About what?"

"About why you need *that.*"

When Yuri used that mild-mannered tone, Roman could

hear a big brother lecture coming on. "It's been a long night."

"Since when did that ever bother you?"

"Since this is the end of a big case and I'm bushed."

Roman carried a glass and the bottle over to the table. They both sat down opposite each other.

Yuri reached for the bottle and set it on the floor. "I'm not buying it. Let's talk about Brittany Langford."

Just hearing her name made Roman's stomach clench. "Why? Tonight I closed the book on her case."

His brother shook his head. "Once upon a time I thought you carried a torch for Angela. But after what I saw go on between you and Brit at the airport, I realized two things. You're in love with Brit, and Angela was never in the running. All this time you've let everyone think you were nursing a broken heart when it simply isn't true."

"Is that a fact." *Dammit, Yuri. Don't say any more.*

"My mind's been going at warp speed all night. I figured that if you didn't leave New York because of her, then you left for another reason. I also figured that since you're willing to walk away from the woman you've fallen in love with, then that means you're in to something that owns you."

Shut up, Yuri.

"About four this morning I asked myself what force or power could rule your life so exclusively, you'd go against nature.

"Around five, the answer came as clear as a bell. I don't know why I didn't see it years ago. Here I was, looking beyond the mark when all the time it was right in front of me. It's always been in front of me. You're an agent."

Putting on the greatest acting performance of his life, Roman lifted one eyebrow. "And you're full of it this morning."

"I haven't worked out which branch, probably CIA." He kept on talking as if Roman had never said a word. "From the time I taught you how to crack a safe when you

were just twelve years old, you always did imagine yourself
a spy.''

Big brother—you've outdone yourself this time.

''It must have happened while you were in the military.
You believed all that cock and bull Green Beret stuff and
went for it! If you had confided in me, I would have told
you not to bother. You'd only end up being disillusioned
because you couldn't right our corrupt world like you did
when we were kids playing at being grown-ups, fighting
the common enemy.''

*You're right, Yuri. It wasn't anything close to what I'd
fantasized about in my teens.*

''I realize you can't tell me anything, but your silence
condemns you. Besides, I see the truth in your eyes. So
why don't you get out before it's too late? There's more
adventure and excitement in marriage than you'll have ever
experienced in the CIA, or whatever it is you've joined.

''Roman—don't you know you're going to age too fast
living a double life with no wife, no children, *nothing* to
show for it but the proverbial bullet in your back one un-
lucky day for all of your idealistic efforts? A woman is a
great deal more satisfying to embrace at night than a stan-
dard issue handgun in a lonely hotel room. Especially a
woman like Brit Langford.''

*With your mind like a steel trap, they should have re-
cruited you instead of me.*

Yuri's expression grew solemn as he stared deep into
Roman's soul. ''I know I'm right. What worries me is that
you might pass her up and never know what real joy is all
about. Think on that.''

He gathered the bottle from the floor and placed it dead
center in front of Roman. ''Pretty pitiful substitute.'' Then
he stood up. Over his shoulder he added, ''Don't go to bed
yet. Jeannie and I need a ride out to the airport in a few
minutes. Since there's no reason to celebrate, we're heading
home. I'll tell the family and anyone else I can that Eric
was joking. *More the pity.*''

If you only knew it, you're speaking to the converted, big brother. I'm going to get out, just as soon as I can tell them. Soon, Yuri, you'll be dancing at my wedding.

CHAPTER NINE

"MA'AM? I've brought in the last box, but it's not labeled. Where would you like me to put it?"

Brit was on her knees putting cleaning supplies away under the kitchen sink when she heard the mover. It was one of her last tasks. She'd spent the whole day getting her condo straight once more and was exhausted.

"Just a minute."

She pulled her head out from under the drainpipe and stood up, only to gasp when she saw Roman standing there in a white T-shirt and jeans molding his powerful body, carrying a carton. Her legs started to buckle and she leaned against the sink for support.

His eyes wandered over her face and hair which she'd swept up on her head to keep it out of her eyes.

She looked a complete mess in a well-worn pair of Levi's and an old T-shirt. No lipstick.

It had been four days since that agonizing moment at her parents' front door when she'd had to say goodbye to him. Four days that she'd been a zombie at work, that she'd gone without sleep or an appetite because she was in so much pain over never seeing him again.

"W-what are you doing here?"

"Helping you move in," he murmured suavely, setting down the box. "The men unloading didn't get the word that we aren't married. Since they thought I was your husband, they told me they were through and asked me to sign the work order. I guess I'm so used to the role, I didn't think twice about putting my initials to it. I hope that was all right."

She moistened her dry lips, trying not to stare at him too

131

hungrily. "Of course. You were the one who hired them in the first place. But as I told you the other night, you've already done too much. I can't afford to pay you for any more help."

His sudden grimace told her she'd said something to displease him.

"I'm not here as a private investigator, but as a friend, Brit."

From the clipped sound of his voice, she was very much afraid she'd offended him in some way. It was the last thing she wanted to do.

"To be truthful, I'm thril—" She stopped mid-word as a flush stole over her face. "I'm happy you've dropped by. Honestly. It's just that you work so hard, you deserve a little time off."

The lines in his face relaxed. "Because of the way I make a living—which by now you know all about—helping you get your place in order is like going on vacation."

"Not quite." She couldn't prevent her mouth from curving upward. "You're an accomplished liar, Roman Lufka, but I won't say no to an offer like that."

"Good. But as far as I can tell, I'm too late. Everything looks just as before."

Miraculously the tension between them seemed to dissolve. Maybe she was mistaken, but she thought she saw a gleam in his eye that wasn't there before.

"There are a few more things to do, but the bulk is done."

He studied her features. "What about this box I brought in? There's no writing on it."

She frowned. "I thought I marked everything. Go ahead and open it."

He was so attractive, so fascinating to watch, she forgot she was supposed to be getting her kitchen in order.

"It looks like some canned goods."

"Now I remember. I had a couple of cases of soup. Oh— and a supply of cat food for Tiger!"

"That's right," he murmured quietly. "I'd forgotten about your transient pet." He lifted his head, darting her an unfathomable glance. "Have you seen her yet?"

"No."

She turned toward the sink so he wouldn't see how much Tiger's nonappearance had disturbed her and finished putting the last cans of polish and cleanser away. It was silly, really, but she was afraid the cat might have felt abandoned and had gone off for good.

"Then who's meowing out on your patio?"

Brit whirled around. "Roman—" she cried joyously. "Tiger *did* come back!"

She hurried through the kitchen to the dining room. After drawing the curtain aside, she undid the lock on the sliding door and opened it.

"Is that Tiger?" Roman asked, standing so close behind her she could feel the heat of his body.

"No—" she whispered in surprise, still light-headed from his nearness. Reaching down, she picked up a tiny, furry, striped kitten. "But it looks like it could be one of her babies. Oh, Roman. It's adorable. Look how little it is, how helpless..."

"Well it seemed to know where to come to get love. Maybe your Tiger brought it here."

Brit raised her eyes to Roman. His bent head was only inches from hers. She could feel his breath on her cheek. "Do you think?"

"Stranger things have happened. Someone told me that cats often choose their owners, not the other way around. If Tiger had something to do with this, it was because she knew her baby would be safe with you."

Roman's mouth was too close. She yearned to taste it again. She loved him too much. Swallowing hard, she backed away, the kitten still in her arms.

Out of the periphery she saw his chest heave. "Unfortunately your landlord doesn't allow pets."

He'd just brought up the problem she'd been struggling

with. "I know. I've been taking a chance feeding Tiger. But I couldn't possibly allow this dear little thing to fend for itself."

Already Brit loved it and couldn't imagine parting with it, not when its delicate pink tongue was licking her fingers.

"Oh...she's hungry and I don't have any milk. Do you think she's too little for the cat food?"

"Probably."

He took the kitty from her hands and examined it. "I'm afraid she's a 'he.' What are you going to name him?"

"Clouseau," she answered automatically before she realized what she'd said.

He laughed out loud. The sound reached to that inner core of her. "You mean the *in*famous, ridiculous French Inspector Clouseau?"

Mortified, she gripped his forearm lightly and looked up at him. "Roman—I didn't mean anything by it. You *know* I didn't. You're the antithesis of him, but because you're a P.I., the name just popped into my head. It's an absurd name really."

"Clouseau it is." The impact of his white smile was devastating. "I'm not complaining. For all his bungling, the Frenchman *was* legendary."

Now the kitten was licking Roman's hands, obviously looking for food.

"I have an idea. Why don't we take him to my house? We'll stop at a pet store on the way and get him the things he needs, including a little bed. He can live in the kitchen until he's trained, then we'll go from there."

Brit stared up at him in disbelief. "You wouldn't mind the idea of a kitty underfoot?"

"No. I've always wanted a pet, but because of my work, I couldn't have cared for one properly. To be truthful, it would be nice to come home to something alive and warm, provided *you* come and take care of him when I'm on a case and can't get home."

"Of course I'll come. Every day if necessary." Much as

she loved the kitten, her emotional outburst sprang from the deep-seated desire to be with Roman. Four days' separation had felt like four years.

In her heart she knew she'd pay a heavy price if she became more involved with him, but right this second she didn't care.

"Then it's settled," came the low-toned response.

Brit—you're insane. The whole point was to make a complete break from Roman because he's in love with another woman. Don't get any ideas that he wants to see you!

He's only offering to help you out with the kitty until it's a little older because he's such a wonderful human being. You won't be seeing each other coming and going. If that's what you're hoping, then you're headed for disaster. You're delusional.

"I'm usually home in the early mornings. If you would come after you've finished work, I think we'll have our bases covered." He continued to rub behind the kitten's little ears. "You'll need a front door key. Remind me to give you one when we get home. I'll drive while you hold Clouseau, then I'll bring you back here later. Shall we go?"

"Yes," she murmured, her heart racing in her chest because she was going *home* with her *husband*.

In one short week of living with Roman, that was how she'd come to view him.

As far as his house, it represented home to her. In comparison, her condo felt like a motel. "I'll just lock up and turn off the lights."

By eight o'clock that evening, the kitty was sleeping in a flannel-lined basket in Roman's kitchen. He'd drunk his milk and eaten his kitty chow. Roman had taken him outside, then brought him back in for the night.

Standing there watching him with Roman, Brit felt like Clouseau was their baby, fresh home from the hospital.

They'd picked up a pizza on the way home from the pet store. Brit was so full, she couldn't manage another bite and felt so contented, she wanted to lounge on the couch in the living room. *She wanted to lie in Roman's arms...*

It was time to go home.

She turned to ask him if he would drive her when the phone rang. He excused himself to take it in his study. It seemed like he was always on call, his life not his own.

But she could never begrudge him his line of work, not after knowing he'd taken her case on faith, without hesitation, calming her fears.

Most likely one of the P.I.s was calling him to check in, or to ask for backup. Roman's colleagues were his other family, a specially chosen, dedicated few, who were the real heroes of this world in Brit's mind.

Eric had gone after Glen Baird without thought for his own welfare. As for Roman, his brilliance in masterminding the entire setup with such speed and forethought had saved her life!

She'd already put the first installment of her bill in the mail. But it seemed such a pittance for the return. She had her life, her sanity back. The only thing missing was her heart, which was his, if he but only knew it.

While she waited for him to get off the phone, she wandered into the living room. A stack of photos on the coffee table caught her interest. They wouldn't have anything to do with Roman's work. All his cases were locked away in files in his study.

The pictures had to be personal. Maybe Yuri and Jeannie had left them. *Or maybe they were pictures of Angela.*

This wasn't her home. She had no right to rummage around in his things, but her need to see the woman he couldn't forget, overcame the dictates of her conscience.

Before she lost her nerve, she dashed across the room and took a cursory glance at the top photo.

A small cry escaped her lips. Her hand shook as she lifted it for closer inspection.

Her wedding pictures!

Phil had been the photographer. He'd snapped Roman

seconds before embracing her after Sid had pronounced them man and wife. She remembered the smoldering look in Roman's eyes before his mouth closed over hers. The camera had caught that look of desire.

How could a man only pretending to be in love appear so sensuous and hungry?

Intellectually she knew it had all been an act, but Brit started to tremble as she relived heart-stopping memories, making it difficult to breathe.

She looked at the next picture, then closed her eyes tightly. It was one of her, caught a second before Roman's mouth descended. Phil had captured the image of a woman in love. Had Brit's eyes really blazed such a hot blue?

Quickly she turned to the third picture.

Dear God—the way they were kissing each other, anyone could be forgiven for believing the two of them were passionate lovers.

Am I really the woman in that photo clinging to Roman as if he were my whole life?

"I see you found the pictures."

Roman's low, vibrant voice caused them to slip from her hands. She hadn't heard him enter the living room.

Warm-faced, she knelt down and started to gather them up from the carpet. "I came in here to wait for you and s-saw them on the table," she explained awkwardly.

"I left them out purposely so I wouldn't forget to give them to you. Sid brought them by. Everything to do with your case is yours and has been itemized on the bill so you'll know exactly what you're paying for."

The world started to spin as the tiny hope that maybe he treasured them, too, was snuffed out.

The words were like a dagger plunged straight into her heart.

She got to her feet in a daze.

Jeannie's words came back to haunt her. *Don't listen to what anyone says about Angela.*

Brit took a fortifying breath before putting the pictures

in her purse. She'd made the greatest mistake of her life coming here tonight, agreeing to help take care of Clouseau. But she was committed and couldn't go back on their bargain.

Pasting a smile on her lips, she turned to him. "If you can take me home now, I'd like to get back to my condo. I'm expecting a call from Denise. She and Rod are flying in tomorrow and I'm going to pick them up at the airport."

He nodded. "I would have offered, but something has come up and I have to leave town for a week."

"A new case?" She feigned a bright voice.

"No. Something vastly different. I have to go."

To New York most likely. To *her*.

"Lucky for me you're already planning to check in on Clouseau every day. Would you mind watering the plants one time while I'm gone?"

"Of course not." She desperately fought to stave off tears which were threatening.

A whisper of a smile formed on his lips. "It's kind of nice knowing my wife is going to be around a while longer to keep an eye on things while I'm gone."

"Ex-wife," she amended, needing to get away from him as fast as possible, before the pain exploded.

"You have to be divorced to wear that title," he said over his shoulder as he headed toward the door leading to the garage from the foyer.

She followed a few steps behind. "Since we were never married, it's a moot point." Brit had to say it, if only to convince herself.

"How did I fare as a bogus husband?" he asked, opening the car door for her.

Her pain translated to anger. She bit out, "On a scale of one to ten, a perfect twelve."

Before he shut the door he said, "Which leaves me to wonder about my score if we had been legally wedded."

Don't say any more, Roman. It's killing me.

He levered himself behind the wheel. "Why so quiet?"

"You haven't mentioned *my* score."

"We'll talk about it when I get back."

Oh, no, we won't!

"Denise? It's Roman Lufka."

"Roman— You're back! Brit said you'd be gone a week, but I guess your business took longer than you'd planned."

"I returned as soon as I could," came the vague explanation. *The process had taken more like ten days. But I'm free now. Nobody owns me.* "How was Disneyland?"

"It was fine. Thanks to you, everything's *wonderful* now that Glen Baird has been put away for good. My parents and I sent you a check a couple of days ago. They want to meet you and thank you in person. But like Brit says, we can't put a monetary value on what you did for us."

"Thank you, Denise." Roman warmed to her words. "It was all in a day's work."

"Not to us it wasn't!" After a brief hesitation, "Do you want to pick up Clouseau, or shall I bring him over to your house? Whatever is best for you."

He frowned. "*You've* got Clouseau?" An odd prickling raced down his spine.

"Yes." She sounded surprised he'd even asked. "Isn't that why you're calling? To pick him up?"

"How come you have him?"

Another silence ensued.

"Didn't Brit tell you?"

"Tell me what?" he demanded.

"I thought you knew she has a new client. He flew her to St. George to look over some property with him and work up a few preliminary sketches. Since her parents are on vacation, she asked me if I'd take care of Clouseau until she got back."

"That explains why no one answered at her condo," he said more to himself than to her. Roman's disappointment at discovering Brit wasn't even in Salt Lake was so acute, it had caught him completely off guard. The fact that she'd flown off in a private plane with a strange man did nothing to improve his mood.

"How long has she been gone?"

"Two days."

"Do you have any idea when she plans to return?"

"No."

"Do you have a number where she can be reached?"

"No. I'm sorry. Maybe if you called her firm, they could tell you."

He took a deep breath. "It's too late to phone now."

"Roman—if you just got back, would you like me to keep Clouseau another night? It would be no problem."

"No, no. I'll come and get him now. Has he been good?"

"He's been perfect. Brit practically fell apart when she had to leave him."

That night in the kitchen he'd witnessed Brit's reaction to the tiny kitten for himself. He'd investigated a dozen ads for new kittens until he'd found one that resembled Tiger. If she could give that much love to an animal, then he could only imagine the affection she would shower on a newborn baby. But not just any baby. *His* baby.

Yuri was right. There was no substitute for family. "One of your own, little bro. Remember, you're not getting any younger." That's what he'd told Roman after Roman had left headquarters in Virginia to spend a night with his brother. Finally he was able to confide to him that he'd left the CIA before flying back to Salt Lake.

It came as a crushing blow to discover Brit wasn't anywhere around. His eagerness to see her had turned into an ache that wasn't about to go away. Since it looked like he was going to have to bide his time until her return, he'd have to make do with Clouseau's company.

Of course he didn't have a lot to go on. Roman knew enough about women to realize she liked him, but she'd given him no overt sign that her feelings for him ran as deep as his.

Out of frustration he'd purposely told her to take the wedding pictures because they were her property. He'd hoped that they meant so much to her, she'd be hurt that he'd simply pass them on to her without any indication that they were important to him, too.

When he saw the blood drain from her face and felt her frozen silence, he was filled with an elation he could scarcely contain. At least she wasn't indifferent to him. But he couldn't do anything about it until he'd resigned from the agency.

That was ten days ago. He'd returned a new man, only to discover that she was in St. George with a male client. When he'd heard that news, a surge of unprecedented jealousy consumed him.

No matter how absurd, Roman felt totally territorial where Brit was concerned. Except for a legal piece of paper, she was his wife in all the ways that counted, *but one*.

He hadn't realized his emotions could be so savage. The thought of another male hanging around her, getting close enough to her to start a relationship was making him a little crazy. He could imagine the other guy touching her, holding her...

Every time he relived her passionate response to his wedding kiss, his desire for her burned that much deeper. His need had grown to the point that he had a good mind to camp out at her condo until she walked through the front door.

After being terrified for over a month, it would probably frighten her if she found him there, which would be the worst thing he could do on the heels of the stalking case. But since he'd thrown away the mask, he was running out of patience to remove hers.

A much better idea would be to ask security at the airport in St. George to call him as soon as she showed up with her client for the flight back to Salt Lake. All Roman had to do was give them a description of Brit, and they'd have her spotted in one second flat.

The minute he knew her arrival, he could have her tailed and know exactly when she drove over to his house to take care of Clouseau. After the way they'd parted last time, he surmised she would attempt to come when she thought he wouldn't be there.

If I put Eric on it, you won't stand a chance, sweetheart. This will be his opportunity to make amends for the mischief he caused, and play cupid for real at the same time.

The three day trip to St. George had lasted longer than Brit had wanted, but it couldn't be helped. It was ridiculous to worry if Roman had returned to Salt Lake when it didn't matter. She had no intention of seeing him again.

On the flight home, she decided that as soon as she could reach him, she'd tell him he could keep Clouseau. If he told her that it was impossible because of his schedule, then she'd take the kitten back and keep the knowledge of it from her landlord. But this business of going over to Roman's house had to end.

Of course he might be gone weeks. Enough time to be with Angela again, whatever the situation. He was so vague about his private life, Brit had no idea of his plans, but it was absolutely essential that she avoid bumping into him again. He would put two and two together with the result that he'd end up pitying her for her obsession with him. *An insupportable thought.*

Their fake marriage had meant about as much to him as a plate of day-old baked beans left uncovered. She had her pride and wasn't about to let him see that he'd managed to turn her world upside down.

With that settled in her mind, it came as a shock after arriving home in her car from the airport to learn from Denise that Roman had returned the night before and had taken Clouseau home with him. Because of Angela, she'd somehow imagined he'd stay longer.

Hurrying into the condo with her suitcase, she took a shower and fixed herself some soup for dinner. When she tidied the kitchen, she reached for the phone, intent on contacting Roman and getting this over with.

He was probably out on a case, but she would give it a try. Even though she was terrified to talk to him, she couldn't put it off any longer.

To her amazement he picked up the receiver on the second ring and said hello. Always when she heard his deep male voice, her body trembled. Now she was breathless and sounded like a fool when she finally found her voice.

"Hello? R-Roman?"

"Welcome home, Brit, or are you calling from St. George?"

She bit the underside of her lip. "No— I'm back." Trying to calm that fluttery feeling in the pit of her stomach she said, "How was your trip?"

"You could say it has made a new man out of me."

She blinked in shock. "You sound happy."

"I am," came the low, resonant reply. "Probably happier than I've been in years."

He and Angela must have gotten back together.

Her heart was on the verge of breaking. "I'm glad for you. I don't know another person who deserves personal happiness more than you." She cleared her throat, needing to change the subject. "Roman—about Clouseau—"

"He's doubled in size while I've been away. I didn't recognize him. Amazingly enough, he recognized me. The little guy has acted very pleased to be back on his own turf."

"I imagine it's because he's chosen you for his owner."

"Not quite. Maybe you haven't noticed it yet, but you left your blue cardigan sweater on the chair seat in the study when you moved back to the condo. Whenever I can't find Clouseau, he's lying on top of it probably wondering where you are. So far I haven't had the heart to remove it."

Roman. I wish you hadn't told me that. I'm already shattered at being apart from you. This pain is never going to go away unless there's a complete break.

"That phase won't last long. Pretty soon he'll be prowling for mice. Roman— I'm designing a new complex of condominiums in St. George and will have to be down there quite often for a while. It's going to take a lot of work and I won't be able to keep regular hours.

"Starting tomorrow, I can't even promise that I can come by your house, not when I have to maintain such a different schedule."

There was a deafening quiet on the other end of the line. Girding up her courage she continued, "I think we need to decide which one of us is going to keep Clouseau. If you don't feel you can be there for him enough of the time, then I'll take him to my folks until I've finished with this latest project. Mappy, their last cat died, and I think Clouseau would fill a void. But that's only a last resort."

"I'll keep Clouseau with me," he replied in an even tone. "When I can't be here, I'll ask the woman who occasionally does housecleaning for me to look after him."

You should be happy now, Brit. The operation is over and all ties have been severed. Tell him you have to go and hang up.

"I—"

"Congratulations on your new commission—" he broke in. "It sounds important."

She drew in a shallow breath. "It is. I might even make enough money to send you a lump sum toward the balance I owe you."

"Am I such an ogre that paying me back is all that occupies your mind these days?"

She'd made him angry when she hadn't meant to. "Of course not, Roman. I guess I'm still in a daze because I don't have to be afraid anymore. If you've never been in my position, then you can't possibly know the depth of my gratitude for what you did. I'm truly sorry. I won't bring up the subject again."

"I'm going to hold you to that," he ground out.

The fury in his tone unnerved her. No matter how wonderful he was, she would never want to cross him.

"I'd better go. As it is, I'll probably be up all night working. I'm glad Clouseau has found a home with you." Her words were coming out so jerky, she could sense tears threatening.

"Thanks again for everything, and g-good luck in the future."

"You took the words right out of my mouth."

The line went dead.

She replaced the receiver with a hand that was shaking. "Okay—" she cried out to the empty condo. "That's it— You've just seen the last of Roman Lufka. Now what are you going to do with the rest of your life?"

The answer was too horrendous to even contemplate.

"I've got to get out of here."

She grabbed her purse, locked the front door and took off in her compact car without a destination in mind.

A half hour later she found herself traveling up Emigration Canyon, her tears spent for the moment. Salt Lake was getting toward the end of September and it was cold out, especially in the mountains. She shut the window and turned on the heat.

The lights from the family owned café which had been there forever twinkled up ahead. When she saw a bunch of cars parked in front, she decided this was exactly what she needed—a place full of people and music from the jukebox.

After walking inside and ordering a hot chocolate, she changed her mind about staying. A couple of husky, college-age guys spotted her immediately and began making pests of themselves. She had the suspicion they'd come in here with too much to drink already.

She left her mug half full and turned to go. They started to follow her out the door. That was all she needed, she groaned.

"Don't leave!" they called to her. "Come on back and let's get acquainted."

"Sorry. It's my bedtime." She hurried down the row of cars where she'd parked hers on the end.

"Mine, too," one of them interjected. "Hey, beautiful—why don't we go together?"

"Sorry," she called over her shoulder. Brit had assumed they were pretty harmless, but when she heard footsteps directly behind her, she wasn't so sure.

"You can't walk out on me now, baby."

"*The lady just did.*"

Brit gasped out loud and swung around to see Roman who'd insinuated himself between her and her pursuers, stopping them dead.

CHAPTER TEN

THE forbidding expression on his face made even *her* body quail. This was an entirely new facet of the man she loved. A tall, dark, cool and collected modern-day warrior who was awesome to contemplate. Especially when he was wearing a black turtleneck under his dark brown leather aviator jacket.

The world reeled for a moment. *How in heaven's name had he happened along?*

When the answer came, she felt even more light-headed. He had to have followed her up here. *Why?*

"This is none of your business. Get out of the way!" the one closest to her challenged Roman.

In a lightning move, Roman displayed his ID. "Police. Turn around and put both hands on the car. You, too." He motioned to the guy further behind. He spoke with unquestioned authority. She noticed they didn't give him any more trouble. *He's magnificent.*

"Ma'am," he muttered, not looking at Brit. "Please get in your car on the passenger side and stay there till I give you permission to do otherwise."

Passenger side?

She swallowed hard, doing his bidding without question. In this mode, she wouldn't have dared defy him. For the first time since she'd known him, she was seeing him the way those on the wrong side of the law would perceive him. *No* person in their right mind would dream of disobeying him.

"You have the right to remain silent." She heard him read them their rights as she shut the door and turned the key in the ignition so she could put down the window.

Now he was speaking into his walkie-talkie, calling for backup. In utter fascination she watched him frisk and handcuff them. They were so drunk, they each had to lie against the trunk of a car or they would have fallen in the dirt.

Deadly methodical, Roman approached their car and began examining the inside. While she sat there shivering from an inexplicable fear coupled with a heightened sense of excitement, she heard the mournful wail of a siren getting closer.

Soon lights were flashing and everyone in the café came outside to see what was going on.

With incredible calm, Roman told everyone to get back inside until further notice. His demeanor brooked no argument from a single soul. She knew he carried a weapon, but he hadn't used it.

Steel inside the velvet glove.

To Brit, Roman was bigger than life.

You're not only in love with him. You're in awe of him. You always will be.

Within five minutes two police cars had converged and the young men's arrest was under way. Brit watched Roman converse with one of the officers, then he turned in her direction. In a few swift strides, he swallowed the distance between them.

A tight band constricted her breathing when he got in the car and revved the engine once before backing out onto the highway. As they drove off down the canyon she thought she saw Eric in one of the company cars. He must have brought Roman to the café.

"R—Roman?" she ventured when she couldn't stand the tension-filled quiet of the interior any longer.

"You have the right to remain silent, to obtain legal counsel. Remember that anything you say can be held in evidence against you."

"*Roman*—" she cried out incredulously, but he refused

to answer her or even look at her. "You're frightening me."

"You need to be frightened," he bit out. "Maybe it will teach you not to go alone in places like that this late at night."

"But it's a café!"

"As you've just found out, it's a favorite haunt of the drinking crowd from the university. It's raided on a weekly basis."

Brit didn't know that and she'd lived here all her life. "But they wouldn't have hurt me. They wouldn't have dared with all those other people inside."

"You mean all those others who were equally inebriated?" That little nerve was throbbing in his temple again. "For a woman as sophisticated as you are in some ways— you're still amazingly naive in others."

"Thank you very much," she retorted, stung by his criticism. She would have said more but he was speaking into his walkie-talkie again, this time to Eric, telling him that he was on his way home and would get back with him in the morning.

Brit could only assume that Roman meant for her to drop him off before she drove home.

"Why did you follow me?"

"If there's to be any interrogating, I'll be the one to do it. Right now I think it would be better if neither of us said anything."

She didn't know Roman like this and couldn't imagine what she'd done to make him behave this way. His formidable mood drained all desire to provoke him. Instead, she stared out her side of the car window, but the passing landscape remained a complete blur.

Roman lived so close to the mouth of the canyon, it only took a few minutes to reach his house. Like *déjà vu*, they entered the garage, then got out of her car and went inside.

Their footsteps must have alerted Clouseau. Brit could hear him meowing from the kitchen, but Roman had closed it off. Needing comfort from any source to counteract this new form of pain Roman was inflicting, she started in that direction until his words stopped her.

"We'll leave him there for the time being. Shall we go into the living room?" It was a demand cloaked in the politest of questions.

Brit's heart accelerated to a wild rhythm as she followed him through the foyer to the familiar room where she'd spent so many hours dreaming about him, fantasizing about a future together while she waited for him to come home from work.

She'd been a different woman then. The client he'd sworn to protect. He'd been her savior.

Tonight he was her abductor, and she his captive.

As he shrugged out of his jacket, revealing the superb musculature of his hard body the black turtleneck and trousers only enhanced, a strange thrill of anticipation mixed with apprehension spread through her being.

She'd left her condo without a coat. He kept the heat down. Now she was feeling a little cold and vulnerable. She wished she had something to cover her off-white cotton sweater and jeans.

Taking refuge in one corner of his comfortable leather sofa, she curled up, clutching the arm nervously with her right hand.

He stood a few feet away from her, his powerful legs slightly apart, his hands raking his hair. Then he stopped, and they dropped to his sides.

"Why did you lie to me tonight?" he began.

Alarmed, she cried, "I don't know what you mean."

"You told me you were inundated with work—a new project that made it impossible for you to come over and do your part for Clouseau."

Her cheeks started to flame. "I *do* have work."

"Really. Then how come a thorough search of your condo produced no evidence to substantiate your claim."

She froze. "*You were in my condo tonight?*"

Ignoring her question, he fired another one. "You said you were going to be up working all night. Yet the second you got off the phone with me, you were out the door like a shot."

Brit's eyes grew huge. "You had me tailed!"

"Were you supposed to meet someone at that café?"

The change of subject confounded her. "No— I just stopped there because I got cold and felt like something hot to drink."

"Do you always leave your condo on a flying run with no regard for the temperature outside?"

"I refuse to answer any more questions when you don't answer any of mine."

If he'd been in her condo, that meant he would have seen things she'd never meant for him to see.

His eyes darkened so that hardly any green glinted through. "I didn't know you had any. Fire away."

Now's your chance to hear the truth, Brit.

"Where did *you* go for a whole ten days?"

"Unfortunately, that's classified."

She stifled another groan.

"Is that it?" he baited.

"No. How can you stand there grilling me when every time I ask you a question, you either change the subject or tell me it's confidential. You sound just like a mob boss always pleading the fifth amendment."

He grinned. "I like your analogy."

Furious with him she said, "But I'm an open book, and because you're a P.I., you can enter my condo with or without my permission and there's nothing I can do about it."

"That's right. Unless you want to start telling me the truth."

"About what?"

"About the reason why you have the picture of us kissing, set in a frame at the side of your bed."

She couldn't swallow or breathe. "I—I thought you were

a gentleman. How mistaken could a woman be." To her horror, her voice quavered.

He flashed her one of his disarming smiles. "I told you up the canyon you're too naive for your own good. By the way, I'm waiting for your answer."

She had to think fast. "I always keep souvenirs of the important incidents in my life."

"I suppose that will do for starters."

"That's all the explanation there is, Roman."

He shook his head and moved closer. "I don't think so." He reached the couch and sat down next to her, encircling her shoulders with his arms so she was imprisoned. "I think you've been lying awake nights wondering what would happen if we finished that kiss we had to break off for propriety's sake."

"*Propriety's sake*?" she whispered, too bemused by his nearness and the enticing tang of the soap he used to think with any coherence.

"Hmm...you know as well as I that if we hadn't had an audience, it would have gone on and on."

"Roman." Her voice trembled. "Please don't do this."

"I have to."

His expression sobered, then she saw the banked fire in his eyes and her insides turned to liquid.

There was no way to escape his grasp, no place to run. But when she felt his mouth close over hers, she found she didn't want to escape. His kiss blotted out all cognizance of her surroundings. The sounds of Clouseau's meowing faded. Everything. *Except* the thunder originating from her heart.

This was what she'd wanted, what she'd craved long before they'd become man and wife. Roman's mouth was sending her into shock and she welcomed it, returning each devouring kiss with a passion that had transformed her.

Something amazing was happening inside her, as if she recognized that this was the experience she'd been waiting for all her life, this explosion of need that drove her to undreamed of heights and feelings only a man like Roman could create.

"I want you, Brit." His deep voice shook with desire against the scented flesh of her throat where his lips worked their magic. Too euphoric to realize what she was doing, she wrapped her arms around his neck in response.

"Roman—" she cried his name on a low moan, offering herself up to him in a surrender of soul as well as body.

The taste of him, the strength and hardness of his virile body had brought her own femininity to staggering awareness. The realization came that never again would she be complete without him, without *this*.

Overwhelmed by needs bursting out of control, a shudder of ecstasy passed through her body and she clung to him shamelessly.

"I'm right here, darling," he said against her lips. "I'm not going anywhere and neither are you," he murmured with a primitive fierceness that thrilled her and seemed part of the whole divine sensation which was overpowering in its intensity.

He leaned over her, raining one soul-destroying kiss after another on her face and cheeks, her gleaming blond hair which splayed over his strong arm.

Brit's breath caught at the raw blaze of hunger igniting his eyes. "I wanted you the moment you walked in the police station," he confessed huskily. "I wanted to take you to bed the day we were married. I want you now and *know* you want me."

His chest heaved from the strength of his feelings. "You know what I'm asking, don't you, Brit?" His mouth descended once more, sending her reeling into a world of sensual pleasure more exquisite than before.

Drugged by needs which were fast growing out of control, she was barely capable of cognitive thought. She was in a precarious situation because more than anything in the world she wanted to know his possession.

But she wanted a lot more than that. *She wanted to belong to him. Forever. Legally and binding.*

But did he want that, too, or was physical assuagement all he could give because he'd lost his heart long ago?

He was kissing her again with such hunger, she could be forgiven for thinking he was laying heart and soul at Brit's feet.

She needed clarification. He hadn't once used the word love. He'd been very careful *not* to use it.

His way of being honest? His way of letting her know exactly where she stood?

Brit wasn't a naive schoolgirl. She'd had enough years of experience to realize a man could become involved in a totally physical relationship, but remain emotionally detached. It happened all over the world, every day, with millions of men.

When the relationship ended for whatever reason, they moved on to a new woman without ever looking back, leaving the other woman behind, emotionally devastated. In some cases, never the same again. Brit in all probability would be another casualty of that particular group.

Unfortunately, the old cliché was true about a man's love being a thing apart, but for a woman, 'twas her whole existence.

Brit could choose to ignore that fact. It would be so easy when she was painfully in love with Roman. She could give herself to him. It would be the transcendent moment of her life.

But she knew herself too well. There would always be nagging pain and uncertainty when he left her bed. In time, it would drive a wedge between them because she wanted all of him. In the end, she would want more than he could give, and he'd move on.

"Brit—" he urged her to answer him, capturing her mouth in a surge of longing, the caress of his hands tangible evidence of his growing need.

She wanted to succumb, to find forgetfulness no matter

how ephemeral, but at the last feverish second she cried, "Did you say these same things to Angela when you were in New York with her all of last week?"

Angela?

Having Brit in his arms at last, tasting her mouth to his heart's content, memorizing the look and feel of her beautiful face and body had enchanted Roman to the point of no return. *Or so he'd thought.*

On a shudder, he slowly relinquished his hold of her and got to his feet. He'd been so enraptured, he hadn't realized that they'd been lying together on the couch.

Inhaling lungfuls of air, he stared down at her, rubbing his neck absently. Judging by the fire singeing her cheeks, she, too, was beginning to realize just how far one kiss had taken them.

Though there had been women in his past who knew from the beginning that he couldn't give them a commitment and understood that fact, nothing in his experience could describe the way he felt about Brit.

She had become the embodiment of his every need and desire. He didn't have to fantasize—not when she inculcated the best of everything in a woman and was physically perfect to him.

His eyes closed tightly. Someone had been telling tales out of school, and it wouldn't have been Yuri. It meant that Jeannie had been the one to do the damage.

"What exactly did my sister-in-law tell you about Angela?"

Brit stood up jerkily and put some distance between them. In a frantic gesture that turned his heart over she attempted to smooth her disheveled hair and straighten her sweater.

"You did it again, Roman," she said with an edge to her tone. "You answered my question with a question. Either you've been in law enforcement so long you don't know how to carry on a normal conversation, or the subject of Angela is off limits.

"In any case, I'm not prepared to sleep with a man who can't be totally open and honest with me, no matter how wonderful you are."

Brit, darling—

"Until I met you, I couldn't have fathomed making love with a man before marriage. That tells you how besotted I've become over you. It's the reason I've tried to stay away from you, though in truth I do have a lot of work to accomplish this next month."

"Brit—"

"No!" She cut him off abruptly. "I'm not finished. You wanted answers so you're going to get them. There's something you should know about me." Her eyes flashed blue sparks.

"I'm such a poor loser I've always wanted to be first at everything—my studies, sporting competitions, my career, men...

"Second best will never be good enough for me. You had your chance to tell me where you've been for ten days, but you didn't take it. You had the opportunity to answer a straightforward question about Angela, but you chose to avoid a simple answer in that inimitable style of yours.

"So now I don't want to hear what you have to say. It doesn't matter what Jeannie told me."

Roman could feel her slipping away from him and he started to get the slightest bit apprehensive. "Angela's married."

"What does that have to do with anything?" she retorted so fast, he was dumbstruck. "In ways, what you've just told me makes everything that much worse!

"You may be every woman's fantasy, Roman—even mine," she admitted through gritted teeth. "But that's all you'll ever be!"

"What in the hell are you talking about?" he demanded, at a total loss for an explanation.

Instead of answering his question, she made a dash for the foyer. By the time he could compute that she was actually running out on him, he heard the garage door open and she was backing out.

Jeannie Lufkilovich, what in the name of heaven did you tell Brit?

Not wasting a breath, Roman jumped in his BMW and backed out right behind her. After trailing her to an obscure café up the canyon, he couldn't second guess where she might be headed now. But one thing was certain. He would have this out with her tonight no matter where they ended up.

At the light near the freeway he saw her glance in the rearview mirror. He flashed his brights in acknowledgment.

When the light turned green she sped away, her tires screeching as she climbed the off-ramp to the freeway. He followed in hot pursuit, feeling an adrenaline rush the likes of which he'd never experienced before.

The woman he loved beyond description was running away from him. Until he caught up with her and they worked out all the misunderstandings, his life would be a living hell.

At the thirteenth east exit she turned off unexpectedly, no doubt intending to drive to her parents' house. He couldn't allow her to reach it.

Pulling out his walkie-talkie from the glove compartment, he got in contact with his P.I.s, attempting to determine who was closest to them.

Phil indicated he was at a drive-in on seventh east and fourth south, but he could beat Brit to Federal Heights and block the entrance to her parents' driveway.

Roman told him to take off, then stepped on the gas, hoping to rattle her. But when they reached Reservoir Park, she did the unexpected again. She pulled over to the side and came to a complete stop. She even had her window rolled down by the time he approached her car.

"How come you decided to make this easy for me?" His voice grated as he placed both hands over the opening.

"I saw you calling for backup."

One dark brow lifted in amusement. "Maybe you should become a P.I. in your spare time. You're developing the instincts of one."

"No." She shook her ash-blond head so the silky mass danced around her shoulders. "That job is definitely reserved for hero-types."

Roman grimaced. "We're going to call Jeannie together and find out what she said that turned the most beautiful night of my life into a nightmare. We can do it at my house or yours."

She'd lowered her head so he could only see a partial profile. "There's no point, Roman."

Sucking in his breath he said, "There is if you're in love with me, and I happen to believe you are."

With that remark her head flew back and he captured her tortured gaze. "Do you deny it?"

Her classic features hardened. "That's confidential, Lieutenant."

He deserved that, but he was feeling too out of control to calm down. "So hardball it is. Have you made up your mind where this three-way conversation is going to take place?"

She looked away. "I'm going home."

"Excellent choice. I'm right behind you."

Ten minutes later, after he'd apprised Phil that his services were no longer needed, he pulled in the driveway behind Brit's car.

When he entered her condo, he could hardly believe she was the same woman who'd hired him because she was so terrified of her stalker.

All fear had left her. In its place was a defensiveness that absolutely baffled him. In truth, it was starting to terrify him.

While he undid the cover over the phone connection and attached another wire from his own phone, she stood in the middle of her kitchen, arms folded.

He punched in his brother's phone number, then handed

her the other receiver. He felt the trembling of her fingers as she took it from him and reluctantly lifted it to her ear.

"Hello?"

"Hi, sport."

"*Uncle Roman*!"

"How are you doing?"

"Great. I hope you're coming to visit us. Mom and Dad are really worried about you."

"Is that right. Is your mother there?"

"Yeah. Just a minute and I'll get her."

Roman's eyes narrowed on Brit's face, reading the question in her eyes. "That was Robert, aged nine."

"*Roman*? How's my favorite brother?"

Jeannie's exuberant voice almost knocked him over.

"Hi, Jeannie. How are you?"

"Better now that you've called. Yuri's going to kick himself for going to the store."

"That's all right, because it's you I wanted to talk to. Tell me what you said to Brit about Angela."

There was a pronounced silence. Then, "Did I say something I shouldn't?"

Roman's hand tightened around the cord. "No, of course not. I'm just curious. I think she must have misunderstood what you meant. Do you recall your exact words, or an approximation?"

"I—I think I warned her not to listen to any gossip about your leaving New York because of her."

Covering the mouthpiece he whispered to Brit, "Is that what she told you?"

After a second, Brit nodded before averting her eyes.

"Anything else, Jeannie?"

"No." She hesitated. "Oh... I don't know. I was just so excited to think you two were married, I was babbling."

"That's okay. You've told me enough."

"I'm sorry if I've caused you any problem."

"You haven't. I just needed confirmation. Thanks, Jeannie. I'll call soon."

"Roman— Please forgive me if I said or did anything wrong. You know how much I love you and want your happiness."

"I do, Jeannie. I love you, too. Say hi to Yuri. I'll call soon."

"Please do."

He clicked off and undid the cord, fastening the cover back in place. Then he took the receiver from Brit and hung it up.

"She was right, you know. If we had been married and you had heard gossip about me and Angela, that's all it would have been. Gossip."

That comment brought her head back up. "She said other things, Roman."

"Jeannie admitted that she did. What else? That she married my best friend, Frank?"

If anything, Brit's face went a little paler. "No. Frank's name wasn't mentioned. She said your brother supported you in your decision to move to Utah because he knew what you were up against."

Roman was thinking hard... "So you assumed from everything Jeannie said that I left New York with a broken heart because the woman I loved married my best friend."

Brit's eyes were half-veiled. "Did you love her?"

"Yes."

She didn't move, but her eyes darkened. "Did you leave because it was too painful to be around them?"

"No. But that's what everyone else thought, even my brother."

"Are you still in love with her?"

"No."

"Why did you break up?"

"Because I wasn't in love with her."

A frown marred her delicate brows. "But you just said you loved her!"

"There are many degrees of love, as you know. Being

in love is a completely different proposition." He could hear her mind turning everything over.

"I-if it wasn't because of Angela, why did you uproot yourself from family and friends to live in another part of the country where you would have to start all over again?

"I know how much you love your brother. Jeannie said it almost killed him when you left."

He put his hands on his hips. "My sister-in-law really did babble."

Brit ignored the comment. "You're not a cruel person, Roman, so it doesn't make any sense."

"It did at the time."

"But you're not going to tell me the reason for the move, or where you spent the last ten days."

"If I told you that neither has anything to do with another woman, what would you say?"

She searched his eyes. "I'd say you're entitled to your secrets. They have nothing to do with me."

"But they do, more than you think."

"Roman—" She let out a sigh. "You're being cryptic and I don't understand you. Please. I—I think you'd better go."

Anger and frustration warred for supremacy. "Why? You don't want me to."

"Actually I do. You're a fascinating man and I admit I'm attracted to you, but I can't handle secrets. When I came to you as a client, I told you everything important about myself. I had to, so you could protect me.

"But you didn't have to tell me anything. All I needed to know were your credentials listed in the Yellow Pages. A man who has been where you've been, and has done the things you've done, naturally has a past. I don't even know how old you are and—"

"Thirty-eight—" he rapped out.

She was retreating further and further from him, like a drowning victim going down for the third time and he couldn't reach her.

"Please don't misunderstand me, Roman. I don't mean to sound critical or jealous. But you admit you're holding something back. The fact that it doesn't have anything to do with a woman makes me even more nervous."

Roman couldn't believe what he was hearing. "Go on."

"Something tells me you're involved in matters that I don't even want to know about."

I was right about you, Brit. You have razor-sharp instincts.

"What has made you come to a conclusion like that?"

"For one thing, the first night you came over to my condo, you told me information about Glen Baird that the investigating officer *and* Lieutenant Parker said might take weeks to investigate.

"But you had all those details at your fingertips within a matter of two hours or less! No ordinary P.I. would have that kind of information, even if you *had* worked for the New York City Police Department."

The hairs were standing on the back of his neck. "What are you getting at, Brit?"

She stared at him through wounded eyes. "Just that you seem to have amazing connections at your fingertips. Too amazing, *unless* you're an undercover agent of some kind. And if that's the case, I don't want anything more to do with you."

Her words chilled him.

"You have an extraordinary imagination."

She shook her head, her features looking chiseled. "You see? Your conversation isn't even normal. You're a professional at something. I have no idea what, but you're simply too good at what you do for your talents to be wasted in Salt Lake.

"In all probability you had to move from New York because of some top secret reason, so you were planted in Utah."

Roman smiled, astounded that she had devined so much about him with that intelligent brain of hers and didn't even know it. "I think you missed your calling as a spy novelist."

"If so, then you're providing the copy," she fired back. "It's been in all the papers about the way you commandeered the stakeout of the Moffat brothers in Nevada.

"But it wouldn't surprise me if you were involved in training those Afghan freedom fighters out in the Nevada west desert!"

How did she know about that?

"I happened to come across an article about it from a speech made at one of those political luncheons which had been put on the Internet." She read his mind, obviously too keyed up to stop talking. "Apparently some Green Berets were involved."

"Green Beret?" he mocked, his heart pounding too fast.

"Yuri told me all about your exploits so don't attempt to deny it."

"Have I said anything?"

"No," she retorted, the color in her face intensifying. "You never do. You let people say whatever they want about you, make assumptions about you, and you never bother to defend yourself one way or the other.

"Only someone highly trained for covert operations learns to dissemble the way you do."

He almost choked. "Covert is an interesting choice of words."

"It's an ugly word, one I hate."

For the most part, so do I, darling. That's why I got out.

"Have you finished writing my obituary?" he quipped, attempting to inject a little levity into a conversation that was starting to chew him to pieces.

"You can make light of this all you want, Roman, but it's obvious that's what you are. Otherwise you would be married by now. You're not that different from your brother."

"That's a real compliment, Brit. I love him."

She nodded. "I noticed. They were both so disappointed

when I told them we weren't married, you would have thought they were attending a funeral. It's what I thought when I witnessed their reaction."

Roman could just imagine.

"Tell me something, Brit. I'm curious. When did you start thinking all these incredible things about me?"

"Incredible, but true, Roman," she persisted. "I don't know. Maybe when I saw that picture of you on the mantel in karate gear. You were a little old to be training for a black belt unless you had intentions of actually incorporating it into a hidden lifestyle."

"That fertile mind of yours knows no bounds." *It's one of the things I love about you, Brit.*

"Maybe you tipped me off when you told me about the family business, or possibly when you said you were the black sheep. The more I think about it, you've been dropping clues all over the place. But I was too focused on my fear to pick up on everything until now."

"And your conclusion?"

Her chin lifted. "There's no man to compare to you, but I'd rather give up men altogether than contemplate a relationship with you."

When she meant business, she went for the jugular.

"Assuming that what you've been thinking was true, which I'm not admitting or denying, am I so hateful?"

"Of course not, or I wouldn't be standing here having this conversation with you," she bit out heatedly. "But what you do is hateful because you don't live a *real* life. One would never know at any given time whether you were playing a role, or being yourself. I would imagine that you yourself get confused sometimes."

You imagine correctly, my love.

"Every time you had to leave me to take a phone call, or get in the car, or take a plane, I would never know where you were really going, what you were really doing. Your friends could be your friends, or they could be other operatives. You could be in danger, killed, eliminated, and I wouldn't have a clue.

"There'd be some trumped-up story about what happened to you. An accident. The whole thing would be covered up as if it had never been."

The pit in his stomach was enlarging. "So marriage to such a person would be out of the question."

She shivered visibly, wounding him all over again.

"Marriage implies home and family," she said woodenly. "I wouldn't dream of bringing a child into the world under those circumstances. For one thing, if your cover were ever blown, someone could come after your family in retaliation. My child could be snuffed out or kidnapped—" Another visible shudder passed through her beautiful body.

Exactly my reasons for never taking a wife, besides the fact that I never did meet a woman I wanted as much as I want you, Brit Langford. Whether you say so or not, I'm going to have you.

He lounged against the counter, crossing his legs at the ankles and folding his arms. "Well, now that you have that all worked out in your mind, it appears you wouldn't marry me or even consider having a long-term relationship. So how about spending the night with me."

"No thanks, *James*. Try Ms. Moneypenney. Make all *her* dreams come true, instead."

He flashed her a smile. "Ms. Moneypenney's mind doesn't intrigue me as much as yours."

She glared at him. "I would be out of my mind to consider a one-night stand with you."

"Not even if I beg?"

"That doesn't deserve an answer."

"Whatever happened to the client who said she'd never be able to repay me for all I did for her," he baited mercilessly.

Her eyes glittered dangerously. "Am I to presume that you'll take what you want because you have all the power on your side?"

Roman felt her question like a bullet wound to the heart. "You honestly think I'd do that to you?" he ground out with barely controlled fury.

She stood her ground, not flinching. "I don't know, do I? You had me tailed tonight. You let yourself in my condo without permission. You possess every gadget to monitor my comings and goings, listen to my phone conversations. You carry a weapon and know moves they taught you in the Marines that would prevent any pitiful defense of mine. No doubt you have keys to the front and back door as well as my car.

"No one would question your right to do as you please around here because everyone thinks we're still married. I'm well and truly caught in your grasp, if that's your intention."

The scenario she was painting made his blood chill because in theory, she was right. An unscrupulous monster might take advantage of her, given her beauty and vulnerability.

"I think you've been watching too many spy videos."

She rubbed her palms against her hips in an unconscious gesture.

"I think you'd better go."

"After a character assassination like that, I'm surprised you bothered to make the suggestion."

"So am I," she whispered brokenly. "Please, Roman. Just leave."

He straightened to his full height. "Before I go, let me leave you with a couple of thoughts. First and foremost, I'm in love with you, the only contingency your overactive imagination didn't think of."

She stared back at him with a stunned expression. *Good.*

"Second of all, you have nothing more to fear from me. I left all keys on the table next to our picture by your bed. I've debugged the condo. There's nothing left to show that we ever knew each other, except for Clouseau, of course.

"When I walk out this door, you're on your own. I suggest you hire someone to make your place burglar proof, but that's up to you. What surprises me is that with a creative mind like yours, you didn't see to it when you first moved in. Take care, Brit. See you in the movies.''

I'm giving you twelve hours to come to your senses. If I haven't heard from you by then, I guess I'll have to talk to someone higher up so I can make my final and permanent move into your life.

CHAPTER ELEVEN

C AND G Surveillance Products turned out to be an enormous building with so much inventory, Brit was staggered. It was like being lost in the British Museum or something.

"May I help you?"

Brit jerked around anxiously. "I hope so. I'm here to see Mr. Lufkilovich."

"I'm sorry. He took a late lunch and probably won't be back for a while."

"If it's all right, I'll wait."

"Of course."

Brit turned from the counter displaying all the latest locksmithing tools and wandered over to a shelf loaded with transmitter detectors and sound amplifiers.

The need to discuss everything with the person closest to Roman had driven Brit to take a morning flight to New York.

After that desolating moment when Roman walked out her door last night, she'd been on the phone in tears for a good portion of the early hours with Denise. After discussing everything, Denise agreed that Brit needed answers only Yuri could furnish.

Since Brit was out of money until payday, Denise offered to put the airline reservation on her credit card. Like the good friend she was, she also drove her to the Salt Lake airport.

It had been a mad scramble to get ready, to call Mr. Dunlop's answering machine and inform him that she'd had to go out of town for a few days on an emergency. Denise volunteered to tell Brit's parents that she'd be away from the office, but would call them at the first opportunity.

Adrenaline had been surging through her veins since her plane had arrived at Kennedy. Coupled with no sleep, she was a mass of nerves and looked worse, all puffy-eyed and drawn.

If she was wrong about Roman, then she didn't know how he could possibly forgive her for the things she'd said, practically accusing him of being dishonorable when he'd been the epitome of everything she'd ever considered decent and essential in a real man.

He'd told her he was in love with her!

Those were the happiest words she'd ever heard. But if she was right and he led a double life, how could they possibly have a future together?

"Mr. Lufkilovich is back from lunch. Whom shall I tell him is waiting?"

Brit wheeled around to face the female clerk. "Brit Langford."

She watched the middle-aged woman speak into the phone before motioning to Brit to go through the double doors at the end of the store.

After thanking her, Brit headed for her destination, but she didn't have far to go because Yuri suddenly appeared with a beaming smile on his handsome face.

He gave her an affectionate, heartfelt hug. "I thought maybe I was hearing things when Cybil told me you were out here waiting. Where's Roman? I have a thing or two to discuss with my little brother."

"H-he didn't come," she stammered. "In fact, he has no idea I'm here and I'm going to beg you not to tell him."

Like before in Roman's living room, she watched his smile vanish. "Come on in my office and let's talk. Cybil?" he called out. "Bring my visitor a cola, will you?"

"Sure thing, Yuri."

There was an understated elegance about Yuri's office that reminded her very much of Roman's taste in decor and furnishings. Oddly enough, she felt at home with his brother and knew she could discuss anything with him without him being critical or judgmental.

Once she had a Coke in her hand, and Cybil had shut the door behind her, Yuri sat back in his swivel chair eyeing Brit soberly.

"Something serious has happened, or you wouldn't be here. How can I help?"

The kindness, the compassion was too much for Brit who broke down sobbing. Yuri immediately supplied her with tissue and hugs until she could get hold of her emotions.

"I f-feel such a fool, Yuri. Please forgive me for doing this."

"I detect Roman's handiwork. Tell me what's been going on."

"No—you don't understand. Roman's been wonderful, and he said h-he was in love with me, and all I did last night was accuse him of being a secret agent."

A strange quiet ensued, alerting her that maybe she hadn't been wrong after all.

It was a devastating sensation, as if she were on a downward spiral headed for heartbreak. Not even Yuri could save her.

"Whatever caused you to think that?" he asked in a low voice, reminiscent of his brother's. If she closed her eyes it was almost like Roman was in the room.

Brit stared at Yuri for at least a minute.

"Things."

The one word answer reverberated in the room. Not surprisingly, he didn't question her further.

"Is it true, Yuri? I have to know."

His eyes were shuttered. "Did Roman deny it?"

"He didn't say anything. I did all the talking. Then he left, a-and I'll never see him again." Her voice was shaking all over the place.

"Is that what he said? Goodbye?"

She nodded. "I didn't give him a choice. I told him anything would be better than having a relationship with man who can't tell me the truth about where he has been, who can't call his life his own."

A shadow crossed over his distinctive features. "I'm sorry, Brit. Jeannie and I had hopes that you and Roman would work things out."

She sat forward, her mouth so dry she had to take another drink. "How can we work anything out if there isn't total honesty between us?"

The enigmatic expression in his eyes told her nothing. "All I can do is give you this." He reached in his top drawer and pulled out a book. "Read it on the plane when you fly back." He opened the cover and wrote something with his pen. "Be assured that no one will know you were here, or that we ever talked. All right?"

What on earth? Yuri was being so mysterious. With heart hammering, she took it from him and put it in her purse.

"When do you fly back?"

"My ticket is open because I didn't know how soon I'd get to see you."

He nodded. "There's a late-afternoon flight to Salt Lake. I'll put you on it myself."

"Thank you, Yuri." Her heart swelled with gratitude for his concern.

"My pleasure. As far as I'm concerned, your marriage was valid and I consider you my sister-in-law, whatever happens. Let's get out of here and head for the airport to make certain you get on that flight."

Two hours later Brit hugged Yuri goodbye and boarded her jet. When the plane had reached cruising altitude, she opened her purse and pulled out the book he'd given her.

"*No Regrets.*" She mouthed the words quietly to herself. *A true story by Conrad Noonan, ex-CIA.*

Intrigued, Brit turned to the flyleaf, curious to see what Yuri had written, but there was no writing. Only the blurb from the publisher.

CIA agent Conrad Noonan's soul-searching journey to find himself took him from the jungles of Vietnam as a decorated Marine, to South America, to the Kremlin, to Beijing, to Israel and Palestine. Each assignment revealed corruption at the highest levels, and all roads led home to the bowels of an even more corrupt group at the White House.

Travel with him along his journey of disillusionment—agonize and thrill with him as he reaches his turning point and gets out of the CIA with *No Regrets* while he can still call his soul his own, while there's still time to claim the woman so long denied him.

She blinked. This had something to do with Roman, but he couldn't have written the book. It had a 1980 copyright. Roman would only have been twenty years old.

Yuri had underlined the entire second paragraph.

Brit read the marked passage again. Suddenly illumination filled her being. Yuri knew the truth! This was his way of telling her *Roman had gotten out of the CIA*! Otherwise he wouldn't have hoped that she and Roman could work things out.

She pressed the book to her chest, tears of joy streaming down her cheeks.

"Thank you, dearest Yuri. Thank you."

She reached up to switch off the night-light. Later she would read the contents. Right now she needed to savor this moment and laid her head back to gaze out the plane window and make plans.

"Denise? It's Roman."

"Hi! To what do I owe the honor of another phone call this soon?"

"Do you know where Brit is?"

"I'm sorry. I don't."

"She didn't go in to work today, and her parents have no idea where she is."

"You sound worried."

"I am. She told Mr. Dunlop an emergency had come up so she wouldn't be in."

"Is her car there?"

"Yes. As a precaution, I let myself in her condo in case she was ill, but there was no sign of her."

"Maybe she had to go out to a site with one of her clients."

"Maybe." He practically growled over the wires. "But it's almost midnight."

"I'll tell you what. If she calls me, I'll get in touch with you. Where will you be?"

"At my office. I've been here all day!"

"Ok. Give me your number. I'll phone you if I hear anything."

"Thanks, Denise."

Roman got the dial tone, then phoned Sid. "Any sign of her?"

"Nope. I've cruised past her house a dozen times."

He inhaled deeply. "Keep cruising!"

"Got ya."

After clicking off, he contacted Phil. "What did you find out at the small airport?"

"No one matching her description has been seen all day or night. Sorry, Roman."

"Just keep on the lookout."

"Right."

Roman levered himself from the chair to pour himself a cup of coffee. *Where in the hell could she be*?

He shouldn't have left her alone last night. She was too upset. He should have stayed there and told her the truth. "Secrecy be damned!" he exploded to the empty room.

The other P.I.s were all out on other cases or he would have sent them in a dozen different directions to locate her. For another half hour he paced the room, then decided to go home. Clouseau needed to be fed.

En route, he informed Sid and Phil where he was going,

consciously searching the faces in every car in the hope he might spot her. It was a gesture in futility, but he felt desperate.

In the distance he heard sirens and shivered because it reminded him Brit could be in trouble. What if she needed help? *Dammit, Brit! Why didn't you tell someone where you were going?*

He turned the corner onto his street and was so deep in tortured thought he didn't realize that a police car behind him was flashing his lights for him to pull over. Another one passed in front of him so he'd be forced to stop.

What in the hell?

Roman decreased his speed, then stood on his brakes and got out of the car. Four officers converged on him at once, their hands on their holsters.

"What's going on, gentlemen?" he demanded icily.

"May I see your driver's license, please?"

Enraged, he pulled out his ID. "I'm Lieutenant Roman Lufka. What is this all about?"

"Is he the man who broke into your condo yesterday, ma'am?"

"Yes—that's my ex-husband," sounded a husky feminine voice, directly behind them.

Brit?

Roman fell back a few steps, incredulous.

"Where have you bee—"

"All right, Lieutenant," he cut him off. "Turn around and put your hands on the car. You're under house arrest."

"*House* arrest?" Roman didn't know whether to laugh or cry, but he decided he'd better find out a little more before he gave the police grief with a few tricks they didn't know about.

He was frisked, then hand-cuffed. "You have the right to remain silent, to retain legal counsel. Anything you say could be held against you in a court of law."

"I want to see my accuser," he demanded. *Thank heaven she was all right.*

"All in due time, Lieutenant. Get in the back of the police car."

Brit Langford...when I get you alone...

The trip to his house only took two minutes. Out of the periphery he saw Brit drive his car into the garage, then emerge from the front door seconds later. The officers escorted him into the house, all the way to the living room where he was ordered to sit down on the couch.

"Are you going to be all right alone with him, ma'am?"

"Yes, officers. Thank you."

"Good night." They tipped their hats and left.

Everything was quiet except for Clouseau's meowing coming from the kitchen area.

Roman stared up at Brit who was dressed in a soft-looking blue cashmere sweater and wool pants. Their color enhanced the blue of her exquisite, dark-lashed eyes. The shape inside those clothes was a living miracle.

He swallowed hard, taking in her flowing ash-blond hair which gleamed in the lamplight.

"Do you want to tell me what this is all about?" he murmured thickly.

"Not yet," she whispered.

As she sat down on his lap, he had this suffocating feeling in his chest.

Without the use of his hands, he was at her mercy. She smelled heavenly.

Her palms cupped his jaws and she gazed deeply into his eyes before covering his face with feather-light kisses, purposely avoiding his mouth.

This was agony of a completely different kind. Brit thought she knew what she was doing to him, *but she had absolutely no idea.* His body ignited at the first touch of her lips.

"Don't do that," he half groaned as she ran her hands over his shoulders and chest.

"You don't like it?" she asked, biting his earlobe gently.

"Brit—so help me—"

"Shh—" She quieted his lips with hers, but didn't allow him total access. He wasn't going to be able to take much more of this. "I'm in love with you too, darling, but you already know that.

"It's the reason I was so awful to you last night," she murmured against his throat, running her hands through his hair. "Because I couldn't bear the thought of you putting your life at risk. If anything ever happened to you, I'd want to die," she confessed on a little half sob, throwing her arms around his neck.

"That's why I flew to New York this morning, to talk to Yuri."

So that's where you were. Oh, Brit…

"I asked him if you were a secret agent. He didn't say anything, but he gave me a book to read. *No Regrets*."

You're amazing, Yuri.

He felt her nestle against him until he was in literal pain because he couldn't reciprocate.

"Without betraying your confidence, it gave me the answer I was seeking. I swear the subject will never come up again. I'll never pry or beg you to reveal anything. I want to pretend that tonight is the beginning of our relationship.

"Darling?" She lifted her head from his neck, her eyes so haunted, so lovely, Roman could have drowned in them. "Please say you'll forgive me for being cruel to you." She brushed her lips against his, sending his blood pressure soaring. "Promise me that if I free your hands, you won't drive me home and tell me it's all over."

There was real pain and fear in her eyes. "I couldn't stand it if you did that. Life wouldn't be worth living."

Oh, sweetheart. The plans I've made for us. There's a judge waiting in Nevada. Our family and friends are going to be there. All that is required now is our presence.

"Undo the cuffs, Brit."

Terrified because she didn't know what Roman was going to do, she got up from his lap and pulled the key from her pocket.

"Can you turn around?"

"I can do better than that," he assured her, getting to his feet in one lithe motion.

It had been one thing to have him tied and sitting down where she was on an equal footing with him. But it was quite another to stand next to all that hard-muscled strength, knowing that within seconds he'd have his freedom to do whatever he wanted.

If she had miscalculated…

With trembling fingers she inserted the key in the lock and turned it the way she'd been shown. There was a click. In a heartbeat Roman had the use of his hands once more. Brit backed away from him as he tossed the cuffs on the nearest chair.

While he rubbed his wrists he said, "Would you let Clouseau outside for a few minutes while I freshen up?"

That low, controlled masculine voice filled her with increased apprehension. "Yes. Of course."

He walked down the hall ahead of her and disappeared inside his room.

"Oh, Clouseau." Her voice shook as she cuddled the kitty who purred noisily. "What will I do if Roman can't forgive me?"

She let him out and made sure he had more food and water, then shut the kitchen door again and started down the hall to the living room.

Roman stepped out of his room at the same time, blocking her path. In the shadowy light she couldn't see his expression, but felt the tension between them like a live wire.

"If you'll get your purse, we're leaving."

"All right."

The despair in her voice tore him apart. He knew she had misinterpreted him, but after what she'd done to him on the couch—the way he was feeling right now—he wanted to devour her. The only solution was to get out of the house, away from the bedroom, where he could think.

She'd never made love with a man before. It thrilled him

that he was going to be her one and only lover. But she deserved a wedding ring on her finger *first*, the same one she'd given back to him when the case was closed.

He locked up behind her and they went out to the BMW. Afraid he would lose his resolve if he touched her, he let her get inside the car before he shut the door and went around to the driver's seat.

"I went too far, didn't I?" she cried out. "But I was afraid that if I didn't have help to make you stay in one spot and listen, you might never give me the opportunity!

"So I phoned Eric from the airport as soon as I flew in and asked him if he could arrange for some off-duty policemen to pick you up after you left your office. I knew you could have taken them *all* on. But I was counting on your noblest instincts to understand the trouble I'd gone to, a-and hoped you would cooperate until we could be alone."

So now she had Eric wrapped around her little finger.

Roman turned onto the freeway. "I would imagine you're tired. If you want, climb in the back and go to sleep for a while. Two plane trips across the U.S. in one day are a little much for anyone."

"Why would I do that when we'll be at my condo in a few minutes?" That little quaver in her voice almost defeated him in his purpose. Any second now she was going to figure it out.

"Roman—we're going the wrong direction!"

"Very observant of you."

Her head jerked around. "Then you're not taking me back to my condo yet?"

"Does it look like it?"

"Then w-what are we doing? Taking a drive to help me deal with the pain when you tell me you didn't mean what you said last night?"

"You *are* tired."

She jerked her head around. "Where are you taking me?" The anxiety in her voice pleased him.

"You'll find out when we get there."

"Will it take long?"

"Why?"

"Because Clouseau is all alone."

"I've made arrangements so there's no need to worry."

"But as long as I've come back from New York, I should be at work first thing in the morning."

"You told Mr. Dunlop you'd be out of the office *two* days."

"How do you know that? Oh—never mind."

Out of the corner of his eye he saw her bury her face in her hands. Then it bobbed back.

"My parents— I haven't phoned them to tell them I got back."

Roman smiled secretly. "Technically you're no longer in Salt Lake, so it would be pointless. However, Denise will be there to reassure them you're all right."

"Roman— I swear I'll never play another trick on you again. Your brand of revenge has cured me. Please—"

"I was hoping you'd fall asleep, but since you're too overwrought, maybe you ought to read for a while. Do you still have the book Yuri gave you?"

He could feel her astonishment.

"Yes— It's in my purse."

"Did you finish it?"

"I—I didn't even start it. I just read the flyleaf, but it told me everything I needed to know."

"For once, humor me and turn to page three hundred twenty-four. Here. I'll turn on the map light."

"Roman—" She spread her hands. "I promised you that I would never discuss this again."

"Now that you've been to see Yuri, we *have* to discuss it."

"Are you angry with me for talking to him?"

"No," he answered emotionally. "It meant you loved me enough to go to the one person I trust most for answers. How could I be upset about that?"

One covert glance at those glistening blue eyes and he knew he couldn't keep this up any longer.

"I was wrong to have walked out on you last night, but there were reasons." His voice sounded gravelly, even to his ears.

"I know that now," came her mournful cry, but she turned to the page he'd referred to and read the part where the man in the story has come to a personal crisis because he had been keeping secrets from the woman he loves.

Roman sucked in his breath. "But what you don't know is that as soon as I got home, I had to admit the truth to myself. No power on earth should be more important than the sanctity of marriage. God ordained that a man and woman should cleave unto each other. That means there's nothing standing between them. *Nothing*.

"I was awake all night. If my plan worked out, I was coming over to your firm at lunchtime to take you away where I could tell you those things in private.

"But you had disappeared! I couldn't find you anywhere."

"I'm sorry," she whispered.

He grasped the hand she extended and held on tight.

"I'm not. I'm thankful you went to him. You see, Yuri put two and two together before you did. That night at the house he begged me to walk away from it. He could tell I'd fallen in love with you and urged me to reach out for you before it was too late.

"Long before I had met you, I'd already been contemplating such a move, so he could have no idea how ready I was to do just that.

"But then you stumbled on to the truth and I was in a total quandary. Both my brother and the woman I adore knew about my past. It shouldn't have happened. You weren't ever supposed to know about it in this lifetime.

"But falling in love with you made me vulnerable. You changed me, Brit. When Yuri showed up at the airport, he could see what I was unable to hide. The look of a man who has found the woman he wants to live with, grow old with." Now his voice was shaking.

"I spent nine out of the ten days in Virginia settling my retirement affairs. Then I went to New York. I didn't tell Yuri any more than I've told you. What I did do was give him that book. It was the same book I planned to give you, but Yuri took care of that for me."

In a tremulous voice she murmured, "I don't want to read it. I don't need to. You love me. That's all that matters."

There was a swelling in his throat. "So be it. Now—there's another subject we have to discuss."

"Am I going to like it?"

"That all depends."

"Just say it, Roman!"

Her emotions were as enflamed as his.

"How long do you want our engagement to last?"

"*Engagement*?" The small voice gave him a world of answers.

"Umm. We've only known each other about three weeks. Those who profess to know about such matters suggest six months."

A different kind of silence invaded the car.

"Is that what you want?" She sounded scared to death.

"I want what you want." He raised her hand to his lips and kissed the palm. "A woman deserves to anticipate her wedding. Showers and parties and wedding dress fittings. Not to mention getting to know her fiancé, meeting his family, seeing him under all circumstances so she knows what she's getting into."

"But we've already done all those things! In fact I can't think of anything we haven't done exc—"

"I was thinking the same thing," he interjected smoothly. "Of course it's only natural because you've been saving yourself for marriage. Maybe for us, three months would suffice. We could be married New Year's Day, for example."

"But, Roman—" Her breath caught. "I—I don't want to save myself any longer. I think I'll die if you don't make love to me soon."

That makes two of us.

"There's just one problem."

Her body went rigid. "What?"

"I never dreamed I'd be married, let alone to a woman who's never known another man. When I learned that *that* was one of the gifts you were waiting to give your husband, I'm afraid I envisioned myself as that man. It would make me less than honorable to take your gift before I had the legal right. So we've got a real dilemma."

"No, we don't, darling. We could get married right away."

"Be more specific. You mean sooner than three months?"

"I mean this week!"

He pressed on the accelerator. "We couldn't get everything ready that fast."

"What is there to get ready?"

"Brit— I want you to have the wedding of your dreams."

She enclosed his hand in both of hers. "We already did have that wedding. I felt married to you that day. When we said 'I do,' Roman, I meant those words with all my heart. As far as I'm concerned, the only thing missing was a real minister."

"I felt the same way," he whispered, leaning over to press a kiss to her temple.

"Let's get married as soon as possible," she blurted. "Secretly."

"You mean, elope."

"Yes. But it won't really be like an elopement because we've already had the wedding. Of course, your family wasn't there."

Roman chuckled. "But they were in on the honeymoon, so that evens things up."

He felt her gaze searching his features. "Would you like to elope?" she asked timidly.

"If you do. Where? Mexico?"

"Oh, no. That's too far away and would take too much time. If we went to Reno or Las Vegas, we could be married...tomorrow." Her voice lost volume.

"How about two and a half hours instead?"

"What do you mean?"

He smoothed the hair off her forehead, marveling over the perfection of her features. "We've been so deep in conversation, I guess you didn't notice that we're almost to St. George. We should reach Chief Wilson's home in Las Vegas by 5:00 a.m."

"*Chief Wilson?*"

"A good friend and his wife who are going to be our witnesses. His best buddy is a judge who's waiting to marry us the second we arrive. I think we'd better pull into the rest area ahead and make this official."

"Roman!" she cried out in disbelief as he took the exit. "You planned all this! I can't believe this is happening— Tell me this isn't some dream—that I'm going to wake up."

He came to an abrupt stop. "It's as real as we are, darling."

Reaching into his pocket, he put the diamond ring back on her finger. "I've been wanting to do this since the night you returned it and broke my heart."

"I almost didn't return it. You don't know how close I came to begging you to make our marriage real."

He crushed her mouth once more. "Let's never look back, Brit. We've found something far too precious and mustn't waste any more time."

"I agree," she said with ferocious longing, her desire as volatile as his. She was going to be his wife within hours. He'd never experienced this kind of joy before.

"There's a gold wedding band to match your ring. I bought the set when I took your case. Obviously my subconscious mind already knew there was something extraordinary about you, that I'd found my mate.''

"So did mine,'' she murmured feverishly against his cheek. "Otherwise I would have taken you up on your suggestion to call another P.I. But one meeting with you at police headquarters and I felt this quickening inside me that has transformed my life. You *are* my life.'' Her voice throbbed.

"Then come here so we can put each other out of our agony.'' He undid her seat belt and she launched herself into his arms.

"I love you so much, I can't imagine waiting even two and a half hours more to show you.''

The luscious mouth clinging to his added the one dimension that had been missing from his world up to now. It was the only one that mattered.

Her kisses spelled the future, children, companionship and glorious, unending nights of rapture.

Finally wrenching his mouth from hers because he knew he was close to the point of no return, he said, "Less than a month ago I left Las Vegas experiencing feelings of such profound emptiness and aimlessness, I was actually frightened over my state of mind. Then, incredibly, I met you that afternoon and my world has made sense ever since.''

Brit hugged him tighter. "The day we met, I'd reached rock bottom, as well. Marriage and children didn't seem to be in my future. On top of my pain, there was a lunatic after me. When I phoned your company, it was out of sheer desperation.

"Darling?'' She clapped her hands on his face, her heart streaming from eyes shot with blue fire. "I can't believe I'm saying this, but I'm so thankful Glen Baird picked me out of all the women on the tour to torment. Otherwise you and I would never have met. You're so wonderful. I'm so crazy in love with you I think I'm going to burst from a surfeit of happiness.''

His hunger too great, he bestowed one more kiss on her

avid, passionate mouth, then put her away from him. "As I said before, I think you need a little nap. I think I need you to get in the back seat out of touching distance, or this man won't be driving the car anywhere."

Her eyes grew huge. "You mean you actually want me to get in the back seat?"

"Yes, darling. If you knew anything about men, you'd understand. Of course I'm thankful you don't!" he teased in a low voice, kissing the tip of her well-shaped nose before getting out of the car to assist her.

"But, Roman—" she appealed to him when he opened her door.

"Just trust me and do it without argument, Brit. For what I have in mind after we say our vows, you're going to need all the sleep you can get *now*."

"Really?" Her pout turned into a seductive smile that made him groan. "You promise?" she baited him before getting out and climbing into the back seat where she made happy noises because she'd found a blanket and pillow waiting for her.

"I promise," he murmured against those lips which were luring him into deeper waters.

When he finally raised his head, he was almost blinded by a searchlight from a Utah Highway Patrol car which had driven into the parking lot. Its red and blue lights were flashing as well.

"Roman?" Brit cried out in stunned surprise. "What's going on?"

"I don't know, but they chose the wrong moment this time!" he muttered fiercely.

Both officers got out of the car and walked toward him. With the light at their backs, they were mere silhouettes.

"Are you Lieutenant Roman Lufkilovich?"

"I am," he ground out. *What in damnation was going on now*?

"We're to present this to you on behalf of Cal and Diana, all the P.I.s at LFK, Chief Bayless of the Salt Lake

City Police Department, and your brother, Yuri. Eric says
to drink it in health and take the long honeymoon you deserve. Your brother says, may all your problems be little
Russkies."

As they thrust a magnum of champagne in his hands,
Roman's grin broke into full-bodied laughter.

"My partner and I wish to extend our congratulations to
you, and you, ma'am." They tipped their hats to Brit.

"Thank you," came a little squeak of sound from her
end that kept Roman chuckling.

"Of course it's our job to remind you to wait until you
get to Las Vegas to open it."

"Don't worry, officers. We have a pressing appointment
before a judge who is going to make this beautiful woman
my wife. But we'll definitely celebrate with *this* after-
ward."

He handed it to Brit with another hard kiss on her mouth.
"Keep it safe for us, darling."

He raised his head once more. "Will you convey a message to everyone back home?"

"You bet."

"After you thank them for me, tell them I've died and
gone to heaven."

"Will do, Lieutenant."

"Sweetheart? We've arrived."

When he didn't hear a response, Roman turned his head
to peer in the back of the car. Between jet lag and a surfeit
of emotions, she'd finally fallen asleep.

For a moment he simply feasted his eyes on the woman
who was about to become his other half. At ten after five
in the morning, it was still dark outside. All was quiet except for the pounding of his heart.

You're a lucky man, Roman Vechiarelli Lufkilovich.

When he couldn't wait any longer, he got out of the car
and opened the rear door. Unable to help himself, he leaned

inside and kissed her lips. A little moan escaped, but she didn't wake up.

Chuckling softly to himself, he reached for her and gathered her voluptuous body in his arms. He'd done a lot of illegal breaking and entering where she was concerned, trespassing on private property, spying. He wondered if he dared marry her without her being aware of it. If she didn't wake up soon, he guessed he was going to be guilty of that, too, because he had no intention of waiting any longer to make her his wife.

Someone inside the house must have seen him pull in the drive. By the time he reached the front porch of the chief's sprawling ranch-style home, the door opened.

Yuri stood in the entry with the chief directly behind him, a huge grin wreathing his face. "By fair means or foul, eh, little bro?"

Roman smiled back at the brother he loved. "Is everyone here?"

Yuri nodded. "Both families. Even the judge."

"Good. I'm ready."

"You're supposed to carry the bride over the threshold *after* you say your I-do's," the chief commented wryly.

"I thought I'd get in practice. In the movies it looks so easy."

The two men burst into laughter.

Suddenly Brit's eyes opened. He recognized that disoriented look. "Roman?" she cried, hugging him for dear life.

"It's all right, darling. Go back to sleep. When it's time for you to say that you'll love, honor and obey me, I'll wake you up."

He'd carried her all the way inside the house before she came to life with a start.

"You mean we're here?" she squealed.

"We are."

"*Surprise!*"

It shocked Roman how loud a noise nine adults and three children could make. But it was worth all the effort to get their loved ones here ahead of time just to see the joy on Brit's face. The tears in those incredible blue eyes when she finally looked at him with such adoration made this the most humbling moment of his life.

"The feeling is entirely mutual, darling." On that note, he rewrote the wedding ceremony and kissed the bride first.

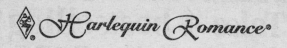

Harlequin Romance®

Get ready to meet the world's most eligible bachelors: they're sexy, successful and, best of all, they're all yours!

BACHELOR TERRITORY

January 1998
Undercover Husband by Rebecca Winters (#3489)
Roman Lufka has been hired to protect Brittany Langford. The easiest way to be by her side, twenty-four hours a day, is to go undercover as Brittany's husband. But the rough, tough P.I. finds himself facing his hardest assignment yet—falling in love!

March 1998
Marriage on His Terms by Val Daniels (#3497)
Nick Evans needs a wife to secure an inheritance. He doesn't need any kind of romantic involvement, so he proposes marriage to the first woman he meets— Shelby Wright. She's shocked, of course, but Nick can be very persuasive.

Bachelor Territory—There are two sides to every story...and now it's his turn!

Available wherever Harlequin books are sold.

Take 4 bestselling love stories FREE

Plus get a FREE surprise gift!

Special Limited-time Offer

Mail to Harlequin Reader Service®

3010 Walden Avenue
P.O. Box 1867
Buffalo, N.Y. 14240-1867

YES! Please send me 4 free Harlequin Romance® novels and my free surprise gift. Then send me 6 brand-new novels every month, which I will receive months before they appear in bookstores. Bill me at the low price of $2.67 each plus 25¢ delivery and applicable sales tax if any*. That's the complete price and a savings of over 10% off the cover prices—quite a bargain! I understand that accepting the books and gift places me under no obligation ever to buy any books. I can always return a shipment and cancel at any time. Even if I never buy another book from Harlequin, the 4 free books and the surprise gift are mine to keep forever.

116 BPA A3UK

Name	(PLEASE PRINT)	
Address	Apt. No.	
City	State	Zip

This offer is limited to one order per household and not valid to present Harlequin Romance® subscribers. *Terms and prices are subject to change without notice. Sales tax applicable in N.Y.

UROM-696

©1990 Harlequin Enterprises Limited

HARLEQUIN WOMEN KNOW ROMANCE WHEN THEY SEE IT.

And they'll see it on **ROMANCE CLASSICS**, the new 24-hour TV channel devoted to romantic movies and original programs like the special **Romantically Speaking—Harlequin™ Goes Prime Time.**

Romantically Speaking—Harlequin™ Goes Prime Time introduces you to many of your favorite romance authors in a program developed exclusively for Harlequin® readers.

Watch for **Romantically Speaking—Harlequin™ Goes Prime Time** beginning in the summer of 1997.

If you're not receiving ROMANCE CLASSICS, call your local cable operator or satellite provider and ask for it today!

ROMANCE CLASSICS

Escape to the network of your dreams.

See Ingrid Bergman and Gregory Peck in *Spellbound* on Romance Classics.

Free Gift Offer

With a Free Gift proof-of-purchase
from any Harlequin® book, you can receive
a beautiful cubic zirconia pendant.

This stunning marquise-shaped stone is a genuine cubic
zirconia—accented by an 18" gold tone necklace.
(Approximate retail value $19.95)

Send for yours today...
compliments of ◆ HARLEQUIN®

To receive your free gift, a cubic zirconia pendant, send us one original proof-of-purchase, photocopies not accepted, from the back of any Harlequin Romance®, Harlequin Presents®, Harlequin Temptation®, Harlequin Superromance®, Harlequin Love & Laughter®, Harlequin Intrigue®, Harlequin American Romance®, or Harlequin Historicals® title available at your favorite retail outlet, together with the Free Gift Certificate, plus a check or money order for $1.65 U.S./$2.15 CAN. (do not send cash) to cover postage and handling, payable to Harlequin Free Gift Offer. We will send you the specified gift. Allow 6 to 8 weeks for delivery. Offer good until March 31, 1998, or while quantities last. Offer valid in the U.S. and Canada only.

Free Gift Certificate

Name: _____

Address: _____

City: _____ State/Province: _____ Zip/Postal Code: _____

Mail this certificate, one proof-of-purchase and a check or money order for postage and handling to: HARLEQUIN FREE GIFT OFFER 1998. In the U.S.: 3010 Walden Avenue, P.O. Box 9071, Buffalo NY 14269-9057. In Canada: P.O. Box 604, Fort Erie, Ontario L2Z 5X3.

FREE GIFT OFFER   084-KEZ

ONE PROOF-OF-PURCHASE
To collect your fabulous FREE GIFT, a cubic zirconia pendant, you must include this
original proof-of-purchase for each gift with the properly completed Free Gift Certificate.

084-KEZR2